The
Cross 2:

Shots Fired

The Double Cross 2:

Shots Fired

Anna J.

www.urbanbooks.net

Urban Books, LLC
300 Farmingdale Road, NY-Route 109
Farmingdale, NY 11735

The Double Cross 2: Shots Fired

ISBN 13: 978-1-64556-323-5
ISBN 10: 1-64556-323-5

First Mass Market Printing October 2022
First Trade Paperback Printing October 2021
Printed in the United States of America

10 9 8 7 6 5 4 3 2 1

Distributed by Kensington Publishing Corp.
Submit orders to:
Customer Service
400 Hahn Road
Westminster, MD 21157-4627
Phone: 1-800-733-3000
Fax: 1-800-659-2436

Also by Anna J.

Novels

The Double Cross
Exposed: When Good Wives Go Bad
My Woman His Wife 3: Playing for Keeps
Hell's Diva 2: Mecca's Return
Hell's Diva: Mecca's Mission
Snow White: A Survival Story
My Little Secret
Get Money Chicks
The Aftermath
My Woman His Wife

Anthologies

Full Figured 15
Full Figured 4
Bedroom Chronicles
The Cat House
Flexin' and Sexin': Sexy Street Tales Vol 1
Fantasy
Fetish
Morning Noon and Night: Can't Get Enough
Stories to Excite You: Ménage Quad

Also by Anna J.

Independent Projects

Lies Told in the Bedroom
Motives 1&2
Erotic Snapshots Volumes 1-6

Acknowledgments

First giving honor to God, I thank you for once again giving me the words and the ideas to finish yet another project. I never thought I would be writing again, at least not for the public. Writing has always been my first love. My first hobby. My first way of expressing my feelings. This is one talent that I am glad I am able to use over and over again. Each book that I write is my gift that I am giving back in thanks for being bestowed such a blessing. This is my eleventh novel on the books. I pray to produce many more.

To my family, thanks for putting up with me being MIA while I worked on this. Between school, work, running two businesses, and writing, I barely have time to commit to any one thing. You all stayed patient and understanding while I worked my magic. I appreciate and love all of you.

N'Tyse, I promise when God paired us up, He showed out. You are the most patient and understanding person I've ever met in the industry. I thank you for your honesty. I thank you for pushing me out

Acknowledgments

of my comfort zone. I thank you for seeing my vision and allowing me to spin things in my own way. The creative liberties you allow are truly appreciated. Your team is amazing. I love all of y'all.

To my readers, you all never let me fade off. Even when I wanted too so badly. Thanks for sticking with me since *My Woman His Wife!* I'm happy that it's still a fan favorite, and I appreciate all the support. And as always, be sure to spread the word!

—Anna J.

Chapter 1

Selah

And Then There Were Two

Friends. How many of us have them? It's such a simple question that should be easy to answer but has so many stipulations that you have to really think about that shit for a while before you're confident you answered it correctly. I'm talking about true friendship, "ten toes to the ground, standing side by side, we in this together" friendship. The ones you never have to have doubts about because you know where their loyalty lies, and it ain't a lie. They have your best interest at heart over their own every single time. The ones you can have around your man and not think sly thoughts because they wouldn't dare cross that line. The ones you have around your parents and they feel at home because your home is their home, and vice versa. Your girls. You tell them all your bullshit, and they never judge you because they did shit just as fucked up or worse alone and with you. Your secret keepers. Your friends.

Well, let me tell you about friendship. I'm slowly learning not to fuck with it. It ain't healthy, just saying. You have to be careful with that shit and read the caution label on the back like a bottle of cleaning solution. Hell, we learned in science class not to mix bleach and ammonia, and mixing the wrong bitches together can prove just as deadly. There are rules to this shit, feel me? It's the Bible as far as friendship goes. Following rules is a must. Those who don't always end up salty as fuck at the end. I found this out firsthand the hard way.

Rule number one: you have to make sure that the level of friendship in your head is the same as what's in the other person's or people's heads. There's nothing worse than a lopsided friendship. This right here is guaranteed to put you in your feelings quick!

Rule number two: ensure that your crew is air fucking tight. The shit for sure needs to be leakproof. No secrets out. No secrets kept among the squad. No spreading rumors with basic bitches.

Rule number three: make sure that shit is consistent across the board because, in real life, bitches don't always want you to be successful. They will low-key sabotage you, the entire time being your biggest cheerleader, and blame you for the outcome of some foolishness like it was really your fault. And maybe it is your fault for not seeing her shady ass for who she really is in the first place. Trust is earned, not given all willy-nilly. They will always show you who they are no matter what they tell you. Actions speak louder than hot pink lipstick on a dark-skinned bitch.

Rule number four: do not gossip about your main bitch with side bitches. Who are side bitches? Them hoes who are not a part of your main crew. Coworkers, neighbors, cousins you see once a year—anyone who doesn't hold a space in your heart is a side bitch, period. However, listen to the tea. There's always some good shit floating on top with the lemons, and just know that, before it was brought to you, some sugar was added to make it extra tasty. You're going to do one of two things with this info. If it's harmful, take that shit right back to the crew so that you can deal with and dead the situation, in that order. If it's useful, tuck it away until you need it. Even your main bitches can be shady sometimes, so always protect your neck.

Rule number five, the most important rule of them all: remember, anybody can catch a bullet. Team included. Protect your heart at all costs, and do not apologize for it. Hell, they will always move accordingly. You should do the same. If they weren't trying to hurt you, there would be nothing to get back to you in the first place.

Trust me on everything I just said. Believe me, you want to. You'll be out here talking that "best friend" crap, ready to pull the trigger and do time in the clink for they ass, and they don't even fuck with you like that. The same bitch you riding for will sell you out like $50 for $100 on an EBT card with her food-stamp ass. What's even more crazy is everybody knows this, even you, but you refuse to believe it. This is your best fucking friend. Why would you ever doubt her loyalty? The one you give your last to because she's never hesitated to give her last to you. Why would you not believe she felt the same way about you that you did about her? The one you stop all conversation about because can't nobody tell you no bad shit about your main bitch. The one who does you the dirtiest. The one you least suspect. You'll soon come to find that taking the time to listen to some of those conversations may be beneficial to your health. Keyword: listen. And then act accordingly.

You'll also find out that the one you stand for is the same one you'll eventually have to dig a hole for. When you stay ready, much doesn't surprise you. However, it will still hurt like hell, and that's when you have to stop and think rationally. Sit still and get yourself together. The burn from that is like nothing you've ever experienced even if you have before. It's a fresh hurt every time because the old friends who are still left know what you've been through and will still do some fuck shit to blow your mind. Sometimes, without a shadow of a doubt, you have to put them down first or they will come get you for sure. Blink and she got your ass. Know it, own it, claim it, and do what's necessary when the time comes. Now is not the time to hesitate for even a millisecond. Shoot that bitch dead in the head, preferably at close range, and deal with the body later. Clean her fucking clock, and don't think twice about it.

For the record, because in reality this should always be at the forefront of your every thought, staying ready is a learned behavior that's in direct correlation with distrust. These hoes ain't loyal, period. This isn't new information either. This is something your gut has been telling you since day one when you met her ass, and for some odd reason you chose to ignore the damn signs. You see how she treats others, so don't ever think your ass is special. Red flags just slapping you upside the head, and you just turn a blind eye to it all. Just stupid. You'll soon come to find that's one of the biggest mistakes you'll ever make, but not the only one. You'll definitely make more mistakes because you lead in love with your hardheaded ass. Love can't fix everything, sis, and you will find out the hard way that the ones you love most are the ones you really have to watch your back around. Those "throw a rock and hide your hands" type bitches. Wolves dressed in friends' clothing. "Kiss your mom on the cheek and kill her child" ass bitches.

"Dig just a little deeper. I gotta be sure this bitch doesn't pop back up on us. We don't need a repeat of what happened before," I said to my girl Skye as we dug a fresh grave not too far from where we put Chase in the ground just a year before. We started to throw her ass right on top of him, but I refused to let him have company even in the grave.

It took everything in me not to dig his dumb ass up and shoot him again. I still couldn't believe he wasn't here with us physically in the flesh. We were supposed to be working on marriage and a baby who looked like us. I still couldn't believe he had the audacity to cheat on me—with my sister of all fucking people. I still couldn't believe I was in love with his now-dead ass. He typically wasn't the type I went for, but I gave him a chance in spite of the fact that I knew better than to fuck with a drug boy. It was the good dick for me. I still couldn't believe this shit even mattered to me as much as it did. *Why the fuck am I not over it at this point?* I made a mental note to discuss these feelings with my therapist on my next visit.

I kept trying to move forward, but I was stuck in this rut I couldn't seem to climb out of. I wasn't really sure I even wanted out. Lately I'd been coming to the realization that, all jokes aside, I'd killed people, people I'd loved, still loved. I'd ended lives, and these motherfuckers wouldn't let me rest. I deserved to feel like this. It was my punishment for the wrong I'd done, which was why I wouldn't mention it to anyone—not Skye, not my parents, not the therapist, not the woman in the mirror. At this point I felt like

I deserved whatever torture came to me. I'm going straight to hell for the shit I've done. You can put your entire check on that and double up.

Wait, let me just clear up something right quick. I personally only murdered three people: both my exes and my sister. All of them were impulse kills because I was in my feelings and triggered by the moment. I regretted them all. Whatever happened to just breaking it off with someone and walking away? Clearly, I always brought a damn gun to the party, and that had proven repeatedly to cause more harm than good. I was a damn monster, even though my therapist and Skye tried to convince me otherwise. As far as I was concerned, I was a demon just walking among the people above the ground. All I was missing were visible horns.

You would think it gets easier living life after murdering people, but each time is harder than the last. You learn a lot about a person once they are gone, but you have to decipher the bullshit to find the truth. You learn even more about yourself, and trust me when I say you are not ready for that truth. That person staring back at you in the mirror is mean as shit. No remorse. No held punches. Throwing every wrong you've ever done right in your face with full force so that you can really feel the impact.

Everybody always wants to tell you what someone said about you when they get mad, but you can miss me with the bullshit. If you didn't feel inclined to clue me in on the spot and stop that convo dead in its tracks, don't try to backtrack that shit months later. You had your cup ready for that tea, only to swallow it and find out that shit is bitter to the taste. You just as shady as the bitch who started the conversation. Shit, a friend once told me that I was hanging out with people who didn't even fuck with me like that. I asked her, as my friend, why did she allow it? If you know the people ain't checking for me, why would you not say anything, but want to tell me years later? The bigger question is, why would any person feel comfortable discussing you with anyone else? Shade check! Neither that bitch who's pouring or the bitch holding the cup can be trusted. Fuck them both.

Oh, another word of advice. When those people call you to tell you something someone else said, stop the conversation, and if you have their number, put them on a three-way conference call. That way, everything that needs to be discussed can be talked about among all involved. It's so easy to lie on a person when they're not there to defend themselves. This takes you right back to rule number four. If a person feels comfortable talking about a person to you, imagine what they say about you when you're not around.

These are the questions you have to ask yourself, and eventually your crew, when shit gets crucial. Don't be like me and ignore the signs, sis. Do yourself this favor, and address that shit immediately. Be careful with those kinds of hoes and keep them extra close. The fact that any random person can go to your "friend" and discuss you candidly is a dead giveaway that the loyalty you thought was there may not be. That they never even brought the tea back to you, and you have to find out from some random-ass person months later, is all the evidence you need to confirm you acted in your own best interest. Best believe your friend is talking about your ass too, and maybe y'all not as friendly as you thought.

Chase hit me close to the heart, and burying him drained me for sure, but this Vice shit hit dead center like a bull's-eye just as hard as Sajdah's murder, if not harder. I'd never thought the day would come when I'd have to put down one of my own again, but it just goes to show that trust is earned, and even when you think you can trust them, you can't. I hated that the people I loved the most kept proving me wrong. The person I grew to love from a child turned out to be a totally different person I didn't recognize anymore. *Why can't folks just act right? Life would be so much easier for everyone that way.*

We dug in silence a little more, and then I boosted Skye out of the hole first. I was a little afraid that she would leave me in there and bury me alive, but once she was out, she immediately reached down to pull me up. Who would know to look for me here if she were to try some slick shit? We were the only two back here, besides the two dead asses. What was stopping her from bashing me in the head with a shovel and burying me in the same hole? No one would ever know the truth, but unlike this one, my folks would hunt me down. Unfortunately, they wouldn't know to look in a self-made hole in the bottom of West Philly behind an abandoned house. These thoughts almost had me trying to climb out of the hole without her assistance, but I knew enough about people to know I couldn't show fear. She would know she had me for sure.

Did I think Skye would do me like that? I definitely felt like she was capable of pulling it off. My heart was telling me that I could trust her fully. She'd yet to make me feel like I couldn't. I didn't want to box her in with the rest, but I didn't think Vice or Sajdah could do me as dirty as they did, and you see what happened to their simple behinds. Both were dead in the fucking ground, and I would have put Skye's ass there too if I had to. Hell, who was I kidding? I didn't trust Skye, and my guard would be up until I was the last one standing.

The first thing I did was make sure both phones that needed to be discarded were still in the hole before she pulled me up. I just needed to make sure for my own sanity this time that Chase's phone was gone for good, and now this phone was gone too. I took a hammer to both of them and burned the SIM cards as an added measure.

At this point it didn't matter who found those phones. You weren't going to be able to do a damn thing with them shattered into a million pieces unless you just had some time on your hands and a steady hand to glue them shits back together. Jealousy will have you doing some crazy shit, and I had to protect myself at all costs in spite of the love I had for her. I was overly cautious these days, and rightfully so. This last year had taken me all the way through the ringer, and I just didn't have the mental capacity for anything else to go wrong. *Throw the whole year away, and let's skip ahead a few years if we can.* I was over it, and I needed these memories as far behind me as possible.

We popped the hood on the trunk and dragged the body out with a hard thud as it hit the ground. She definitely wasn't handled with care like Chase was as I carelessly scraped her body across the concrete. I almost wanted to stomp on her ass again before throwing her in the dirt, but I resisted. Her being dead was far worse than anything else I could do to her now, and stomping her out would just make a mess we didn't have time to clean up. I started to hide her ass in the basement in Tasker Homes and let the rats eat her corpse, but the residents didn't deserve that kind of torture from having to smell a dead body for weeks on end. They weren't the type to snitch over there, so she would have just sat until there was nothing but bones left. Now the worms would feast on her. I hoped she was looking up at her body being tortured the entire time it was in the ground, because she surely went to hell for the life she lived.

It wasn't the fault of anyone in Tasker Homes that she was a snake-ass bitch, so to the ground she went. When we got her to the opening, we rolled her in headfirst, not caring how she landed at the bottom. Her body hit with a hard thud that echoed a little in the quiet of the night, and it looked like it landed in a very uncomfortable and awkward position. Immediately we began filling the hole again, each pile of dirt hitting harder than the last. No words of concern. No prayers for forgiveness or a peaceful rest. No remorse. I got her before she got me. That was the way the game was played.

Once we were satisfied with the filling of the hole, I knew the hole she had placed in my heart wouldn't last long. I hated to have to do this to her, but she begged me for it. Skye knew it too. She forced my hand in this situation when all I was trying to do was elevate us as a unit. Shit, we were the last of the Mohicans. I wanted the very best for all of us, and Skye did too. We came to find out that this one didn't really give a fuck about us. It hurt me to the core that she couldn't see what I was trying to do for her. Unfortunately, I had to give her the same treatment I gave to my ex-fiancé. The only difference between her and Chase was that no one would look for her for long. They would inquire, but she'd be a distant memory in no time. She was from the projects, and down at that end of the world, it's every woman for herself.

Taking the broom we brought along with us, I evened out the leftover earth as best I could in the dark, being sure to sweep away our boot prints as we backed our way up out of the yard and to the car, same as we'd done before. It felt almost routine at this point and actually began to hurt less each time. Heading to Tasker Homes to drop our dirt in the furnace was next on the list as we undressed and bagged everything up before getting into Skye's vehicle.

Now that she was dead, her truck had been smashed days ago at the scrap yard on Essington Avenue after it was stripped of useful pieces that could be sold for cash. The same dude handled that who took care of my sister's car when we needed him to hide that truth for us as well. That was one less thing on the list of shit we had to hide from the law. Hell, I almost hated to crush it considering she used the money I gave her to purchase it. It was in pristine condition, fully loaded and everything, but I didn't feel like being paranoid every time I saw this truck riding by, thinking her scandalous ass came back to life somehow because I sold it to someone around the way. He offered to buy it off me instead of crushing it, but I just didn't want to deal with it. I literally had to threaten to take it to another lot to get him to crush it. Shit, I had people at chop shops that would take this damn car apart in a split second, but I didn't want any parts of this car riding around in these Philly streets. It had to be crushed, and it wasn't up for negotiation.

So I'm sure you want to know what happened, right? Let's just say my hand was forced, and I did what I had to do. I didn't want to, but the way these streets play you have to go get or get got. Greed is a hell of a drug and will have you trying to sell your momma's pussy for a quick buck if you're not careful. It's cool though. Welcome back. I'm not saying I was innocent in any of this, but it's the survival of the quickest. Now let's get into this shit so that you can know what not to do in a friendship. Let's get ready to ride!

Friendship: what you think you have, but possibly may be furthest from it.

Chapter 2

Vice

Moving Forward

When I say I was sick that they found ol' girl in the trunk like that, oh, that shit had me down for the count for days, not eating or sleeping and with the damn bubble guts. Not because she was dead. Hell, I ain't like her ass at all, and good riddance. She was finally gone. We were supposed to have time to hide the body, and I was afraid of getting caught. They were giving out football numbers nowadays for murder, and I don't look good in orange jumpsuits.

I did my part letting Selah know, in my own way, of course, what her darling sister was up to. I was prepared to throw all they asses under the bus if the law showed up. Let me just toss that out there in the atmosphere right quick so that we are all on the same page. I didn't think she was going to kill her, if I can be completely transparent right now. I wouldn't have been able to pull the trigger if that were my sister. She would have gotten her ass beat on sight for sure for at least a good year, but putting her in the ground just never would have crossed my mind. I would've just dotted her fucking i's and never fucked with her again. Clearly Selah had other plans.

I'll go ahead and put it on record that Selah definitely shocked me with this move. I even expressed that to Skye, and we were in agreement that she was going to let her go. I guess we didn't know her as well as we thought we did. Even her killing Chase blew the fuck out of me. I would have taken that nigga for every dime he had and bounced on him. He loved Selah. Greed kept him from doing the right things to keep her. I don't know a man alive who can resist pussy. A bitch can't force your dick in her. You have to be hard and ready to play, and he gave it up willingly every time.

Okay, that's a damn lie. I personally was hoping she would get rid of her ass, but I didn't think shit would get so sloppy afterward. It was almost like we got too comfortable after we got rid of Chase. We thought we had more time, but that shit snuck right up on our unsuspecting asses. They died days apart. I was sure that shit had Selah banging her damn head against the wall on a daily basis. We really didn't have time to process it all, to be honest with you. That shit happened way too quickly, and I wasn't really banking on Sajdah dying after all of this was said and done. If for nothing but her parents, I did not want Sajdah found that way. Real hood booga shit. I was not that kind of person. I know you probably got your face frowned up like, yeah, okay. Think what you want. I know who I am.

I knew it would be too painful for them to bear, and it would have been a little easier had she never been found at all. That way, they could have made up any story in their head about her disappearance that would help them move on in life. Finding the body was so permanent, and the way she was found was so gruesome. Ugh, it was just too much! I didn't necessarily like Sajdah, but I loved her sister and her parents. I did not want this for them. That check you can cash and take to the bank. I was a fucking goon, but I did have a heart for people I cared about. Believe it or not, I loved Selah. I may not have been the best at showing it, but it was true. Fuck you and anybody who doesn't believe me. Everything I did was in her best interest. It doesn't look like it to anybody right now, but there was a method to my madness. I did her a favor by exposing those frauds. Otherwise, they would have continued to play in her face, and I wasn't having that.

I can't even really remember the events around that time. Oh, wait, we were too busy trying to cover our shit up with Chase and somehow dropped the ball. *Who the fuck left the damn car unlocked? And why didn't the shit lock eventually? Don't these new cars got some automatic feature that's supposed to do that shit for you?* I swear all it takes is a lost child to fuck up everything. I wanted to smack his momma for letting him roam the streets by himself. Y'all need to do better with y'all kids, real shit. Damn crumb snatchers. His momma was probably in the house with a dick in her mouth while this little snotnose was out roaming the damn projects probably trying to find something to eat because she sold her food stamps. I hate people! An abortion is free depending on your insurance, bitches. If you ain't beat to be a mom, let them suck that shit out. Or take a quick trip down a tall flight of stairs. Having the baby ain't never kept a man at home. Not in the history of single moms has that shit happened and probably never will. He fucked up the church's money climbing in that damn car and almost had us on our way to the electric chair and shit. *Stupid-ass li'l boy. If I ever catch his ass outside, I owe him an ass whipping.*

So I know y'all bitches looking at me real funny right now. And in response to that, I couldn't care less. Y'all know there ain't no real loyalty among thieves. Let's not forget that part. Was I wrong for fucking Chase behind my girl's back? Maybe the first time, but if it makes you feel better, I'll take responsibility for the first two visits. The first time was an accident and caught me off guard. I wasn't even expecting that shit, and that damn sure wasn't the reason I was there. The second time was just to see if I could get it again, and he didn't even put up a fight for it. All the times after that was on him because he kept allowing me to come back, using his dick as collateral. He got himself killed. We very well could have stopped when we shared sis that night, but he got greedy. Yeah, I kept showing up, but he never not let me in. He got in these guts every chance he got, and not one time was it forced. I was just glad I wasn't the one who got caught up in there that time. I would have been a goner for sure.

I was over there riding his ass just days before, and I still can't find my polka-dot thong I wore over there that morning. I tried looking for it when we went back to paint the next day after killing Chase, but I had no luck finding it and figured he must have trashed it. I was trying not to look suspect as I searched and painted, telling my girls that I was being sure that all of Sajdah's shit was bagged up. They didn't have any other reason to not believe me, and had the thing popped up, I would have just said it belonged to Sajdah. It didn't matter if Selah believed me at that point. What was she going to do? A comparison swatch of pussy hair to see if I came up as a match? Fuck outta here, yo. Sajdah was already on her shit list, so I had my alibi, unbeknownst to Sajdah's whore ass. As far as I was concerned, anything that didn't belong to Selah belonged to Sajdah. Chase had plenty of other bitches in here, but that wasn't up for debate at the moment. Shit, Sajdah took one for the team and saved all of our asses low-key. If it weren't for me staying on my shit, his dumb ass would have had us caught and killed, and I wasn't letting him put me on the other side of the dirt. Fuck that and fuck him.

The shit actually went better than I could have ever planned it when I found out Sajdah was over there, and all of my sins died with both of those unlucky bastards. I'll just put it on record that I would miss fucking Chase. I ain't gonna lie, he had them good strokes. Homeboy definitely knew his way around the bedroom and had complete control of that gorgeous dick he owned. It was a shame that part of him couldn't have stayed behind, but it is what it is. He never pulled the fuck out. If I weren't up on my birth control, he would have easily had my ass cocked and knocked, and I would have easily taken that trip down to the doctor to dead all that noise. I wasn't about to let a quick fuck have me fucked up out here. Wasn't gonna happen. I wasn't beat to be anyone's momma, period.

I wasn't about to do to him what Sajdah did. How do you think he found out she was pregnant with his child? I sent the information anonymously of course, but if nothing else, I made sure he knew what he needed to know. I was not about to let her play in that man's face, and it did exactly what I needed it to do:

break they dumb asses up. Only it didn't last for long. It pays to have a few good friends who work at the clinic. I just so happened to be there getting a basic pussy check, and I saw her come in the clinic while I was on my way to the back. Damn it if I didn't slide my homegirl a few dollars to print that chart. Money speaks louder than any HIPAA violation I can think of, especially in the hood.

I didn't know if she was going to keep it, but when she fell off the face of the earth and Chase started snapping, I knew I had to let him know what was really good with her. It was my idea to send the note to her office for her to come to his house. Otherwise, she would have gotten away with that shit. I wasn't even fucking Chase yet at that point, but I knew I had to make sure he didn't hurt Selah in any way. I thought that would be enough for him to back off Sajdah and give Selah his undivided attention (and maybe me occasionally), but this fool just kept it the hell going with his stupid ass. I had no choice but to send in the hounds. He was asking for it.

As for the money, Selah played in my face with that one. *$20 million, bitch, and all I get is a hundred thousand? I help you bury three muthafuckas, and all I get is a short stack? Wow, bitch. The shadiest of the shade for acting like that toward the one person who rocked with you the hardest.* Many of you are thinking that she probably didn't owe me shit and I should just be thankful for what I got. She didn't force me to bury the bodies, right? The shovel wasn't put in my hand at gunpoint, correct? I could have easily just walked away from it all, right? I did it for the friendship, right? Fuck outta here. When she hit that lick, we all hit that lick. That's the realest shit ever.

She didn't have to ask me to do shit, because that's the shit we do for our friends. Jump right the fuck in, no questions asked. Hell, had I come up like that, I would have just split the shit equally, but that just goes to show what type of time people be on. I didn't even find out about the $20 million from her. Skye's dumb ass let that one slip out after she gave us the money, which led me to believe that she definitely got more than I did. My Spidey-Sense has never lied to me in the past. When both them hoes started talking about opening up businesses and buying stock, I knew the distribution wasn't equal. Both them hoes played me, and I wasn't just going to sit back and let it ride. I deserved just as much as Skye if not more.

I didn't see it as a big deal initially. I figured I'd just come back for the re-up and we'd be good. Selah knew my spending habits were a horrid mess, so I figured she was just rationing out my cut a little at a time so that I wouldn't go broke in a day. I had no idea what I got was all I would get. So to the mall I went.

LV: check. Virgil Abloh: check. Emilio Pucci: double check. I supported the chick Milano Di Rouge. I also gave some coins to Bellargo and Banni Peru just to say I represented Philly. I upgraded to the Infiniti QX80 and just drove slowly through the neighborhood so that everyone could see me. I felt like Ace in *Paid in Full* after he got his money straight. There was no limit. Once this was done, I'd just go hit the cash queen for some more. I put bodies in the ground for her. There was no way she was going to deny me. The secrets I held for her were worth billions, so a few hundred thousand at a time should have been a drop in the bucket. I'd earned it as far as I was concerned.

I need another stack, I texted Selah one afternoon. I was trying to grab a platter from Texas Weiner, but it was either feed my stomach or put gas in the tank, and I needed a way to get there, so the cash I had was going to the whip. This motherfucker, as pretty as it was, only took premium gas, and the fill-up was never less than $75. I didn't even realize my funds had gotten so low until I checked my account that morning. Ten weeks ago, I was sitting on $100,000. Now all I had was twenty-three damn dollars, and that wasn't even a quarter tank in my whip. Where the fuck did all my money go? It was no big deal though. For sure my ace boon coon would lace me again no questions asked. I was her secret keeper. She would definitely look out for the cookout.

Where did all your money go? she replied, to my surprise.

Wait a hot damn minute! Stop the fucking press! Hold the fuck up! Was she counting my coins? *I know she isn't counting my fucking money!* I stared at the phone for at least five minutes before replying, erasing and restarting my reply a good ten times before sending the proper response. Who the fuck did she think she was, questioning me? My mom? My fucking guardian? My damn financial counselor? Why did it matter where I spent the money? She gave it to me to do what I wanted to do. It didn't matter where it went. I needed more, and I knew she had it.

LV. KOP. Vicky. They got it. I responded by giving her a few store names and designers I spent the money on instead of calling her a million bitches. After all, I still needed for her to give me the bread. I couldn't get too nasty with her just yet. I didn't know how many times I would need to hit her up for cash, so I kind of had to stay in her good graces for a little while longer, or at least until my funds were straight again.

My message sat unread for another thirty minutes before she replied. Hell, at this point I would have to settle for a platter from the Chinese store. I went to look in the fridge to see if I could settle for a quick home meal, but there wasn't a damn thing in there but a box of baking soda and half a stick of butter. Texas Weiner closed at one on the weekends, and it was already twelve forty-five. No way was I going to make it, and I was irked. I even looked out the window to see if anyone was on the stoop to drive me up there right quick so that I wasn't using the little bit of gas I had left, but I didn't feel like fucking for a breakfast platter this morning. Their spicy breakfast sausage was every damn thing, and I had been craving it for a few days now. I guessed I'd have to wait until Monday.

Just as I was really starting to lose it, my phone dinged, indicating that I received a payment on Cash App. I picked up my phone, hype as shit, just to be disappointed a few seconds afterward. This ho sent me a hundred damn dollars. Did she forget to add a few zeros maybe? What the hell was I supposed to do with that? There was no way she just slid me $100 like she was letting me keep the change for running to the store for her. The fucking nerve of this bitch.

Stop by my house later so we can talk. I'm out with my family. We should be back around three.

This ho had me chopped and screwed if she thought I would be moving on her time, but it was cool. I'd be there at 3:01 p.m. on the damn dot this time. She definitely had some explaining to do. I didn't know why she and Skye got so funky all of a sudden, but it was all good. We could all play that damn game. I'd be the bitch to report Sajdah's murder for the fucking reward money and bounce on they ass. The only reason I didn't do it was because the ransom was only worth $20,000. I could definitely get more than that from her. That shit was anonymous though, right? I just had to think of a way of throwing they ass under the bus without fucking my own shit up and getting the money in the process. Fucking with me would have her ass in the clink for the murders of Kevin, Chase, Sajdah, and ten other motherfuckers she never laid a hand on. *Let's not do this. I don't have time today.*

Money will definitely show you a person's true colors. It has always been the root of evil in this world.

Meanwhile, I called Victoria's Kitchen for a crab-cake platter. They were all the way the hell on the other side of town, but they were also slow as hell, so by the time I got uptown, they'd have my shit ready.

I wanted to text Skye and ask her for the money, but she was on the same shit Selah was on. Both these hoes definitely turned on me, even though they both kept saying that they hadn't. Surprisingly, I was the only one who spent my bread on designer shit. I mean, they got some shit, but from what I could see, they were both looking at storefronts and trying to build a brand. I wanted a brand too! We could have easily gone in on some shit together. I just wanted to ball out a little bit first. What was wrong with that? Enjoy the fruits of my labor, and then put this work in. Hell, I earned every dime of the money I spent. She never said I couldn't come back to get more. What the fuck did she think I was going to do? They knew me better than anyone in the hood. She had to know I was about to shine on these hoes right quick. Did I really change that much? Or were they always like this, and I was just now seeing them for who they were?

Nah, I refused to believe my girls would dip on me like that. She was just going through a rough time right now, and I needed to practice patience. She did just lose her other half, her twin, her womb mate. She wasn't over that shit, and I would be shocked if she were. Selah was different from me. Selah loved her sister. She did not want to have to kill her. But guess what, she fucking did! I didn't make her do it, nor did I put the gun in her hand and make her pull the trigger. I simply showed her what she needed to see as any good friend would have done. Get you a friend like me. Real shit. I think I deserve a damn trophy for all the secrets I kept over the years. I was a great fucking friend, and everything I did was for the good of Selah. It didn't look like she had my best interest in mind nowadays the way that I had for her. What the fuck was that about? It was cool. I would get to the bottom of the shit when we met up later. She had some damn explaining to do.

Grabbing my Chloe shades from the coffee table, I got my shit together and stepped out the door. My fucking purse cost me $1,700. I barely had eleven cents to carry in this motherfucker. I paid for it in cash, so I could always take it back, but I was hoping I wouldn't have to. Selah was going to come through for me. I just had to give her a minute to readjust. My impatience was getting the best of me, and now more than ever I had to show Selah that she could continue to trust me.

Starting to rush, I ran down to hop in my car. I wanted to be sure I was back in time to talk to Selah. I'd do whatever she needed me to do to get this bread, but I needed to figure out how to get more. No one really knew she had the money but me and Skye. You can't be sitting on that much money and still living in the hood. Well, she lived in the country, so that technically wasn't the hood in a traditional sense, but too many people knew where she was and could put hands on her. Normally people with that kind of money moved clean across thirty states so no one could find them. For sure if her parents knew, they definitely would have packed and rolled the minute Sajdah was in the ground. Selah was keeping secrets from everybody, and that wasn't a good thing. Before this was all said and done, I'd make sure she wished she had moved away. I put that on the last nut I swallowed, and just like that, her ass would be gone.

Chapter 3

Skye

When It's Questionable, Ask Questions

Wait, she did what?

I was on the phone texting with Selah while I looked through swatches and mockups for my clothing line. I decided to rent space at the new Fashion District (formerly known as the Gallery) in Center City Philadelphia. They were turning it into a high-end shopping experience but were also opening its doors to more independent designers in the Philadelphia area. Downtown Philly was starting to get that New York/Times Square vibe that I was really digging. It looked nothing like the Center City we knew as kids. I was excited for the changes and the opportunity, and I was hoping to share in this excitement with my girls. My hope was to launch my flagship store, Philly Curvy, and then eventually take this show on the road with stores in Atlanta and other hot spots. Selah's Rage Room idea was sure to turn Philly on its ass, and we were all going to win once Vice decided what the hell she was doing with her share of the pie. Unfortunately, it wasn't happening as planned, but I'll get to that later.

My son or daughter was doing somersaults in my belly, which had me feeling a little nauseated, and I was trying to control the gagging feeling I was currently having a losing battle with. The last few months had been rough. Just trying to digest everything that happened all while trying to live like nothing happened was killing me slowly. I still couldn't believe Selah actually pulled the trigger. We had talked with Vice, and she said that she wanted to let Sajdah go. Vice and I had that same type of conversation when we weren't with Selah, and we were both convinced that she would let that girl live. Surprised both of our dumb asses, didn't she? That was the first time that I feared for my life. If she would kill her own flesh and blood, Vice and I didn't hold weight in a bucket of water. It just meant that if it ever really came down to it, I'd have to get her first. Hopefully, we would never get to that point. It would kill me to kill her, but she'd be a dead bitch fucking with me. It would hurt, but I would not hesitate to take her ass out. I put that on everything.

I couldn't think of a dick worth dying over, and I felt like Sajdah told her sister everything she needed to know. I felt like she was being truthful with her. She took responsibility for her shit. She even told her how to get the money. Was it fucked up? Yes. Did she deserve to die? Not in my opinion. She could have very well left her broke and bitter. Chase didn't deserve death either, let the truth be told. Dudes cheat. That's what they get into. We women know this. I'm not saying we have to accept it, but we know it going in. Not every dude cheats either, but knowing the life that Chase led, there were bound to be a bunch of bitches in the tuck. She definitely got caught up in the moment, and I know for sure she regretted it. We had yet to really discuss it in depth, but I knew my friend. This shit had her fucked up in the head. She adored her sister. Living life without her was going to be hard for my bestie. It was definitely going to get worse before it got better.

She asked for more money, chile. I'm over it. We told her to either start a business or invest, not give all her money to the damn mall.

I read the text and set the phone back down. Vice did exactly what I thought she would do. She wasn't cut from the same cloth as us. Selah and I had said that many times over the years. She was our broke best friend from the projects who knew how to keep shit lit. There wasn't an entrepreneurial bone in her body. That wasn't what she got into. No matter how hard we tried to convince her that having her own was so much smarter than scamming niggas, she just wouldn't fall in line. You can't make a person change who don't want to change. That was what separated us from her, but it never changed the love we had for her. We just treated her accordingly.

When Selah gave me the second check for $2 million, I knew exactly what I was going to do with it, and I knew for certain that if Vice ever found out how much I really got, there would be an all-out war. Did it stop me from taking it? Absolutely the fuck not. I deserved every dime. Did I think it was an unfair trade? For sure, and I had to find a way to get my friend to see it how I saw it.

"You sure you only want to give her that little bit?" I asked Selah when she called me to her house to get the money. I really wasn't expecting to get so much. She told Vice that she got $20 million from the account, but she told me later that she took an additional $5 million from her sister's account because she knew her parents wouldn't do anything with the money but let it collect interest. They did eventually start to do little shit like upgrades on the house, but Sajdah's room remained untouched exactly how she left it. Their mom went in there periodically to dust and cry, but everything remained untouched. Her death fucked the entire family up. Even their dad looked ten years older since her passing. He was still fine as hell. He just looked worn down from trying to keep the two women in his life from falling apart while maintaining his own sanity.

All this bitch gonna do is shop. I actually put 500 grand to the side for her in an account, because if I give it all to her now, she's going to blow through it. I did send her $100 through Cash App, though.

Not one lie was detected. For sure Vice was going to eat that shit up like Ms. Pac-Man chasing ghosts, but who were we to tell her what to do with her money? I personally would have just made her aware that once the money was gone it was over. *Don't come back asking for another damn dime.* Leaving it open like this would make Vice think one of two things: she had forever access to cash from Selah, or she would have to beg her for money each time she needed it. Both would not sit well with either of them. If she blew through the shit in forty-five minutes, that would be on her. I would have just given her what I wanted her to have and been done with it. I also felt she deserved more than $500,000. How was it determined that I got $2 million, and all she got was less than $1 million? Something about that math didn't sit well with me at all.

On some real shit, it should have just been split three ways. I understood that it was her man and her family, but we all had blood on our hands fucking around with them. Neither one of us ever hesitated to jump in. Not just with Chase, but with Kevin's slow ass, too. I'd been meaning to have a conversation with Selah about it, but I was really just trying to mind my business and get my shit in order. She didn't have to give us anything if we were really going to talk about it. She never forced our hands. We did it because that's what you do for your loved ones. Both ladies were like sisters I never had, and I was willing to put my life on the line for them. I had already, and they had for me as well. Blood has always been thicker than water, but money will dilute and blur the shit out of the lines that are in between.

I knew once she gave me the check that I would never ask for another dime again. $2 million was more than enough for me to get what I needed to live comfortably even if I never opened a store, which was honestly more of a gamble. I never stopped working at my job, and my man still pulled his weight, too. He didn't even know Selah gave me money. Money changes people, and I just didn't want that truth from him right now. Things were going good with us, and I wanted it to stay that way.

Selah, honestly, just give her a million and be done with it. Have her sign an agreement to cover yourself. Don't let a few funky-ass dollars change our friendship.

Our friendship was already changed. Who was I kidding? Shit, she had plenty of money. Even after giving us what she gave us she was still sitting on $23 million! She wouldn't even miss that little bit of money, and her newest business venture was about to make her a lot more. This shit had me frustrated, and I just couldn't hold it in anymore. I wouldn't be a true friend if I didn't say anything. We were supposed to be able to keep it a bean with each other no matter how much it hurt. This shit wasn't fair to Vice at all, and as a friend to both of them, I just couldn't let it go down like this without saying something.

She's lucky she's even getting what she got. She's not as clean and innocent with that Chase situation as you think. Me and you need to have a real conversation. I didn't say anything at the time, but trust me on this, sis. Vice is a fucking snake, too.

Lawd, what the hell was Selah talking about? Okay, so Vice was a little quirky, but a snake? Definitely not with us. She was the first to set anybody straight when it came to us. Okay, so she and Sajdah didn't click. They never did, not since we were kids. In Vice's defense, she took a lot from Sajdah over the years just for the sake of her friendship with Selah. Sajdah would have been dragged with some of the shit that came out of her mouth, but Vice never fed into it. She flicked her off like a flea and kept it pushing, not giving too much energy to their dislike of each other. She just kept herself at a distance, only dealing with her when she had to. At least that was what I saw, but who knew? I couldn't be there for everything. Maybe Selah knew some shit that I didn't.

Selah, I hear you. You know I have you if no one else does, but come on, sis. She got dirty with us.

Even if you just give her the money and dismiss her afterward. You know how Vice is, I tried to reason with her. Selah could be so stubborn at times.

And you know how I am. She's lucky her ass ain't in the ground with everyone else, she replied quickly. I definitely did know how she was, and she knew how we were too. She wasn't the only one in the crew who knew how to turn the fuck up. We busted guns just like she did. Hopefully she wouldn't need a reminder. At that moment I decided to just leave it alone, but I wasn't about to let it go. Clearly, she needed more time, and I understood it. I was almost certain that she would see things my way eventually. Today just wasn't the day.

I hear you, sis. Just hear her out. We're all still pretty fragile right now after everything that happened. I love you, I texted her back, wiping a stray tear from my cheek. If no other time was the right time, this was definitely the time for us to be closer than we'd ever been. This shit was difficult for me. I hated us like this right now. We were supposed to be ride or die, down for the crew, love over everything else. Where was the disconnect? I needed us back solid again. My message sat unread for about five minutes before she replied. That just let me know that she at least heard me, even if she didn't do what I asked.

I love you too, sis.

I knew in her heart she really did. She was in pain still. Healing was not going to be an overnight thing.

She had to want to move forward. She was sitting with a lot of guilt. We all were. Well, at least I was. Vice seemed to be up to her regular shit, but who really knew? It'd only been a few months since it all happened, so who knew how she was really feeling? Where she's from, they don't show emotion. Chicks from the projects are hard as hell. Seems like their hearts turned black from when they were kids. I had faith in our circle though. We would get through this. We had to.

Glad that this baby finally settled down, I hugged my belly and thanked God for this blessing. I needed this. I needed something to make it all right. Closing my laptop, I made my way to my bedroom, where the love of my life was sleeping. He was my wild card and made life a little more worth living for me. Standing in the doorway I smiled at him, sending another prayer up that he stayed consistent. I didn't want to ever feel the kind of pain Selah felt, but he would get the same treatment as the rest if it ever came down to it.

I knew he had about an hour before he had to start getting ready for work. I hobbled over to the bed and crawled my way up until I came face-to-face with the reason why this baby was now in my belly almost seven months later. Taking him into my mouth, I woke him up with the best head ever, looking to get it in before he was gone for today. Even with this man wrapped around me, I still couldn't get my friends out of my mind. Right before giving in to his touch, I made a mental note to go see them both before the week was out. They needed me and I needed them. If we were ever going to be on the same page, we had to get this bullshit out in the open.

Chapter 4

Selah

Protect Your Peace

Those lamps are cute, ma. You should definitely get them.

I was all kinds of irked when that text came through from Vice. I hadn't heard a word from her since I gave her the money, and the next message I got from her was that she needed more? *If I didn't love her, I'd let her starve.* I'm sure you're wondering where the sudden hate came from toward Vice, especially considering what she'd done for me in the past, but when you find out what I found out, your feelings change for the people you love the most.

My fucking sister was dead. Gone. In the ground. Never to celebrate another birthday with me again. My twin was gone! She was the person in the world who looked exactly like me, felt exactly what I felt, and had the closest connection to my heart. Like, I just wasn't for anybody's shit right now. I had my own demons I had to fight on a daily basis. Although she was gone, she still showed up every damn where I went. In my dreams, in the damn mirror . . . I couldn't get away from her. It wasn't in the plan. Seriously, she was supposed to walk away from all of this un-scathed. The plan was to never speak to her ass again, but that didn't mean I didn't want to see her anymore. Be extra careful what you speak into existence. You never know what the universe will throw back at you. This shit was harder for me than people realized.

It'd only been a few months. It was like people were expecting me to be out here acting like my normal self. I'd never been invited to so many parties and get-togethers in my life. I guessed they were trying to take my mind off the loss, but I just wasn't beat for a celebration right now. There wasn't enough alcohol in the world to drown my sorrows in. Ain't a damn thing normal about any of this shit. I killed my fucking sister, I couldn't tell anyone about it, and I had two people I could barely trust keeping my secrets. I deserved everything that happened to me, twice.

Okay, so maybe there was just one person I couldn't trust. Skye had been A1 since day one and had never disappointed me. At least not that I knew of. Never had she given me a reason not to trust her. Sajdah loved her just as much as I did, which I was sure hurt her, too. We both couldn't believe she was actually gone. Vice had always been on shaky ground as far as I was concerned. I should have never fucked with anyone who didn't like my sister. When she thought as kids she was going to turn me against my sister, she had me fucked up. Sajdah didn't think I peeped game, but I was on it like flies on shit. Do not make my sister feel uncomfortable. I knew it was too late to tell Sajdah now, but I made sure to check her ass that day when she first met my sister. We were not for the constant "same face" jokes that everyone wanted to throw out there. We were identical twins. We were supposed to look alike and didn't feel the need to keep explaining the obvious to slow-ass people. Now I was here alone and left to pick up the pieces.

My mom, on the other hand, was losing it slowly. She tried to act like she was okay, but the eyes showed everything. She was sad, depressed, over it, frustrated, mad as shit, and missing her daughter all at the same time. All because of me. That shit ate at my soul just knowing I was the one who caused her this type of pain. She'd asked me so many times why someone would want to kill her daughter, and I really didn't have an answer. Why would someone want to kill Sajdah? Overall, she was a pretty great person to know. Judging by her memorial service, she was loved by plenty. They showed up in droves for my sister. My reason for murdering her wasn't even a valid one. I really let some preventable shit with a dude who could be easily replaced come between us. I just kept seeing the look in her eyes as she pled for life right before I shot her. What the fuck was wrong with me? I definitely earned the stupidest person of the year award for this one.

I tried to keep my mom moving as much as possible, and as much as she allowed. She hadn't been back to work since my sister's body was found. She just couldn't do it. I would never forget the day she finally ventured into the office just to get out of the house, and I had to go get her from her office because she was balled up in the middle of the floor in a crying fit that none of her coworkers could snap her out of. Mentally she was done. Thank God her work family was really like family and completely understood what she was going through. When I walked in there and saw Mrs. Bernice on the floor with my mom, rocking her, and a few of her other coworkers surrounding them to make sure she was okay, I could just feel the love in the room.

These women watched us grow up. We played with their children and gave the majority of them the name auntie. They were our extended family, and it was a loss for all of us. It broke their hearts when she finally turned in her notice of leave, and they even negotiated holding her position for her until she got better no matter how long it took. She just wasn't interested, and we decided as a family that we wouldn't make her do it. Her office manager saw to it that she got everything that was owed to her and put in her paperwork as early retirement instead of an impromptu resignation. She gave that company thirty-six years of her life. They definitely wanted the best for her.

They gave her a retirement party and everything. We spent an entire twenty minutes at the party before she was ready to go. She hugged as many people as she could before she left, and I went to her office a few days later to clean out her desk and pick up all of the accolades that her job had given her for being a part of the team for so long. It was bittersweet for everyone.

I almost broke down as I cleaned out her office, the pictures of me and Sajdah over the years smothering me and making me feel suffocated. Every picture that I took from her board held a memory that I would never forget. Birthdays, holidays, "just because" pictures . . . I missed the hell out of my sister. I held it together while I was in the office, hugging everyone who walked up and stopped by while I packed. By the time I got to my car, I cried for a straight thirty minutes, and I had no one to call to help me through it. This was a horrible-ass feeling. A few times I thought I heard Sajdah telling me to shut the fuck up with the tears, but that was for sure hysteria kicking in.

I finally got myself together enough to drive home, and when my dad met me in the driveway when I got there, I broke down again. I wished I could tell him what I did. That part was hurting me the most. I somehow thought if I could just tell the truth, things would get better, but I also knew that would make shit a hell of a lot worse first, so I held it in and cried it out. He just held me in his strong arms, letting me get it all out, while simultaneously drying his own tears. This shit was a struggle for all of us, and we just hoped that it would get a little easier as time went on.

My dad and I still worked to keep ourselves occupied, because Lord knows we technically didn't have to. We did try staying home with her for a little while, but the sadness drove us back out the door within two to three months respectively. Financially we were set for years. Not one dime was needed, but we needed something besides constant tears. Sajdah's policy was more than enough to cover her expenses considering it was so sudden, and her bank account was ridiculous. Along with the money I got from Chase, and the money my parents already had stacked, we were good. All the money in the world couldn't keep those thoughts from creeping up on you though. Spirits don't need a dime from you and ain't got shit but time on their hands. So we tried to move forward the best way we knew how. This shit was super hard.

My mom refused to let anyone near Sajdah's room. It was like invisible DO NOT ENTER tape was across the doorframe. I was too damn scared to go in there anyway. I thought her spirit might be in there waiting to get me or something. She tried to tell me the truth, and I overreacted. I now regretted it, and I cried every day about it. My mom would go in there and touch Sajdah's things like she was trying to commit everything to memory. She would dust something off, sit on her bed, and cry, in that order. I could hear her tears from across the hall, and it killed me. These tears were from the gut. They had a different sound as the moans of agony escaped her throat and filled the house with sorrow.

The shit stuck to the walls like flypaper, trapping you if you leaned too close. It was horrible to listen to. Some days I wanted to move out just so I didn't have to hear her cry, but my guilt made me sit in that house and listen to the tears that I caused. That, and I was too scared to be by myself at the moment. Meanwhile, my dad and I would hold each other during those times because she wanted to be left alone. So days like today when she actually wanted to be bothered with us, we would jump at the opportunity to do what she wanted to do. Even if it meant picking out furniture that we didn't need.

Slowly she'd been remodeling and redecorating the house. I thought she just wanted a different atmosphere that didn't remind her so much of Sajdah's absence. A few decorative pillows turned into replacing damn near everything in the house, to having contractors come in to see how to redo the entire downstairs. She just kept talking about this "open concept" that all the houses have on HGTV, and it was easier to let her do her thing and stay stuck upstairs than to say no and give her no outlet. She wasn't quite ready for therapy, and we worked with her on that, not wanting to rush her into something she didn't want to do.

I ran my ass right to a therapist because I needed help. It was guaranteed that had I not gone, they'd probably find my body next, dead and full of pills. Not just for killing my sister, but for all the fucked-up shit I did over the years. An entire eighty-count bottle of Tylenol PM chased by a glass of wine would serve as my last meal. I didn't do it, because I knew my parents would never recover from it.

My dad deserved the man of a lifetime award. I didn't know how he put up with us in here, but he did it without blinking an eye. We had some pretty candid conversations over the last few months that really showed me a lot about him. He was always Superman in my eyes, and him allowing me to see him at his most vulnerable just put him so far up on the totem pole, I didn't think there was a man alive who would ever reach him. He prayed for me and my sister. He and my mom wanted to be parents so badly, and once they learned we were on our way, they couldn't contain themselves. They tried for another child after us, but eventually they became content with the double bubble they got with Sajdah and me.

I remember all the stories of how they would take turns holding us and wouldn't allow anyone in the house until we were almost a year old. My father said that our mother didn't want anyone bringing any germs in around her kids. She took off an entire year from work after we were born, and she only worked part-time at her firm until we were almost 3 years old, when she finally decided to go back to work. She often said that she didn't want us in school until we could fully tell her how our day went. They were very overprotective with us around others, when in reality they should have been protecting us from each other. I didn't know what my mom would do if she ever knew what really happened, and unfortunately, she would never get that truth from me.

After what seemed like years in this store, my mom finally picked out two lamps that she loved. She was planning to turn the basement, which was currently only being used for storage, into a personal space for herself. She had already had contractors come in to transition the space. It actually looked pretty amazing down there. She had a bathroom put in, an office area, craft space, and a few other goodies. She saved all of the family photos that we had and donated everything else. She didn't want to look through the boxes because my sister had stuff in there that she couldn't handle seeing. She simply said, "If I haven't used it in all this time, I don't need it." So my dad and I went through it and did as she wished. I went and purchased a bunch of photo albums, and after getting the pictures in order, I organized them in a few photo albums that I planned to put on her bookshelf once it was installed.

Once we finally made it out of the store, we went to grab a quick bite to eat. I didn't know why I let that text from Vice bother me so much. I guessed because I was expecting more from her as a friend. She straight took her check and bounced. I felt like, even at my sister's funeral, she was just too happy to see her gone. Did she really hate my sister that much? I knew they had a little rivalry going on over the years, but I didn't think it was that deep. She just looked so relieved that she was gone. Like some sordid secret died with her.

I couldn't quite put my finger on it, but something with her and this entire thing wasn't sitting right with me. It was cool. I hadn't had time yet, but I was going to eventually make time to look through those tapes I took from Chase's house. I had at least six months' worth of footage that I needed to get through, but I just wasn't ready to really know the entire deal with him. I wasn't ready to see his face alive again. I couldn't stomach possibly hearing his voice, and I never checked if the tapes had audio. Taking into consideration he was already gone, there wasn't shit I could do to him once I found out anyway.

I had to get to the bottom of who had his phone as well. Every so often I would get a text from his number. Someone was on my ass, but who? I got into the habit of just deleting them when they came in, but I never told anyone. What was I going to do? Go to the police and say I murdered my fiancé, and now someone was texting me from the phone I thought I buried with him? That can of worms needed to stay shut tight for a little while longer. I would get to the bottom of it, just not right now.

Enjoying lunch with my family took longer than expected, and when we finally pulled up to my parents' house, it was around four thirty—an hour and a half after the time I told Vice to meet me. If looks could kill, I would have been next on the list. She gave my parents the warmest hug in the world, but when her eyes landed on me, it felt like hot bullets hitting me in the chest. I cringed a little but pulled it together quickly. I said it once, and I'll say it again: I didn't owe Vice a motherfucking thing whether she agreed or not. I didn't move on her time. She moved on mine.

"Vicerean, it's great to see you again," my mother said after their hug.

"It's great seeing you all as well. I was just stopping by to chat with my girl. It's been a while since I've seen my friend," she replied with a smile so fake it damn near made me gag. She wasn't about to gas up my parents with the bullshit, so I jumped in and cut that shit dead short.

"I'll be right in, Mommy and Daddy. I just want to chat with Vice right quick."

My mom gave her another hug, grabbed one of the lamps while my dad grabbed the other, and they made their way into the house. Once I was sure they were out of earshot, I moved the conversation away from the door and closer to the curb in case I had to dog walk this bitch out of here right quick.

"Good seeing you, bestie." Vice smiled at me.

I didn't even attempt to return the gesture. "Meet me Monday at Wells Fargo in Penrose Plaza. I'll have a cashier's check and contract for you by then. I didn't have time to contact my banker today."

"Damn, that's how we doing it now?" she asked with mock surprise on her face.

"That's what you contacted me for, right?" I retorted, daring her to lie.

"I wanted to check on my friend."

Silence. I believed that as much as I believed in Santa Claus. This ho wasn't fooling a damn soul on this side of the park. *Fuck out of here with the fake shit.* I had to control the urge to floor her ass. "So that's why I haven't heard from you since Sajdah's funeral, right?"

"I was giving you time to grieve her murder."

Wow. This bitch was playing hardball, and that gut punch hit hard as shit. All I could do was look at her. I had to keep my tears in check in front of this ho. She would definitely mistake it for weakness, and I would definitely show her that I was really not to be played with.

"You're right. Let me finish grieving. We will catch up on Monday. I'll meet you there when I get off from work. I should be there by four."

"Work? With all that money you got? You must just be doing it to have something to do or keep up appearances. If I were sitting on millions, I wouldn't be working shit but a good dick ride."

Right hook to the chin. The smirk on her face was testing me to the max! She was really trying to take me to another place, but the devil wouldn't get my energy today. Instead of responding, I just gave her a smile and began walking back to the house. This after admiring the new truck she had purchased. I could clearly see where the bulk of her money went. I couldn't wait to give her the rest of this money so that she could leave me in peace.

"Selah, don't be like that," she yelled from the curb.

I didn't even bother to turn around. I didn't need her to see the tears that were starting to form in my eyes. With people like her you can't show weakness. As far as I was concerned, after Monday we had nothing further to discuss.

Word of advice: check your crew, every 4,000 miles like car maintenance if you have to. Not everybody who rides with you is riding for you. Trust your gut if nothing else. It has never lied to you before. Whatever you think you feel, more than likely, it's exactly what you think it is. Don't let yourself talk yourself out of what you think you know, because you already know it to be true. Read that part again.

Chapter 5

Vice

What's Mine Is Mine

I wanted to spit in that bitch's face. She was really playing in my damn face, and I was really not the one to be played with. She of all people should have known that about me. *Play with someone safer. What the hell are you working for when you're a millionaire?* At this point she was just being greedy with her selfish ass. Meeting up with her was a waste of damn time and my limited amount of gas. Maybe she'd forgotten I had the capability of putting bitches in the ground just like she did. She could have sent that information over a text. I waited over an hour just for her to tell me we would meet again on Monday. That shit was stupid on all levels.

Oh, and don't think that contract mention went over my head. What was I signing a contract for? She literally owed me her life. I would sign "Donald Duck" on that bitch before I put my name on a damn thing. Money is thicker than mud, but nothing is thicker than blood. She had me chopped and screwed if she thought she could just buy me off with a few dollars. *That check must about to be fat as shit if she thinks it's enough to get rid of me. All that and I'm still left hungry over the weekend. Shit, I wanted some crabs. I guess I better make the rest of this change last until Monday.* I really didn't feel like tricking out for a platter tonight. I thought about asking Skye, but lately she'd been on the same type of time Selah'd been on, and I just wasn't beat for it. Had I known I wasn't getting any more money right now, I wouldn't have dropped $30 at Vicky's.

When I pulled back up to my house, I parked and sat inside to reflect on the last few months while rotating Chase's phone in my hand. I was tempted to send her another text, but it would be too much of a coinkydink if I sent it now when I just left from there. Selah was definitely smarter than the average bear. I knew I needed to just chill until Monday, but I also knew I needed a long-term plan in place. Selah had been doing a lot of getting lately. It was about time her ass was finally the one to get got, and I was just the perfect person to set it all up.

Turning the phone on, I took a gander through Chase's contacts. Most of the numbers didn't have a name attached to them, or if they did, they were nondescript. A few said things like lawyer, rich bitch, Goon . . . I didn't know what to think of any of it, but it was definitely time I found out. The few numbers that did have actual names I assumed were close to him. I was nervous about leaving the phone on for too long. I was sure someone was wondering what happened to him. People like him don't just fall off the face of the earth. Chase was the man in these streets. Someone cared about him. As hard as he worked to build his rep when he first got here, I knew for sure his team was wondering where the fuck he went.

I didn't leave the phone on long enough at any given time for me to catch a call coming in, but every so often when I turned it on to torture Selah, a stream of old texts would come through. A few were from various people trying to re-up and wondering what happened to their monthly drop. There was always someone named Goon looking for him, begging for him to answer. I was curious to know who that was, but I didn't have the nerve to ask. I knew if this money wasn't saying what I needed it to say on Monday, I might just be hitting one of these niggas up.

Selah needed to know that she could be touched, too. I would straight use some of her money for murder for hire. I'd been in the game long enough to know I didn't always have to be the one to get my hands dirty. Selah really had me fucked up, and I'd be lying if I said I wasn't in my feelings. I thought we were friends. I guess things changed.

I wondered how her parents would feel knowing they had birthed a murderer. No one wants to be the parent of a killer. Lucky for her, I genuinely loved her mom and dad and wouldn't put them through that kind of agony. At least not right now. Desperate times sometimes called for desperate measures. I never knew what I'd do to save my own ass. I don't trust me, so you probably shouldn't either.

The last few months I learned a lot about myself. The first thing I learned was that I was loyal as fuck. How many bitches in your circle would kill for you? I may have gone about exposing them in a reckless way, but my intentions were pure. I made sure I had enough evidence to not have any doubt. Get yourself a friend like me if you don't have one already, and value that bitch. She would go to the ends of the earth for you whether you deserve it or not.

I didn't have anybody else. I loved Skye and Selah like my blood sisters because they were. My mom was out in these streets on some ho shit just like me. Hell, that was where I learned it from. We never had a bond, like most of us who grew up out of the Ville. I came from the generation where our parents had us young. They pushed us out and passed us off to whoever would watch us. While they were out living their best damn life, we were stuck in the fucking struggle learning how to fend for ourselves. The only benefit I was to my mom was I made her eligible for food stamps, public housing, and a monthly cash stipend. Having me did not keep my father around, and at least she was smart enough to stop at me and not have multiple crumb snatchers to further ruin her life.

Now my mom wasn't all bad. I never missed a meal, and she kept me fresh to death. My hair was always done, and I had the latest of everything. Not because she could afford it, but because boosting was her superpower. My mom moved so quick she was like the Flash. She'd walk in a store with nothing and leave with enough shit for me and her to wear for ten days. She'd go from store to store, getting everything we needed from clothes to food. She sold her food stamps most of the time for cash because she stole what we needed to eat more often than not. She also used her food stamps as collateral to get my hair done and shit like that. They did the best cornrows in the projects, and Tanisha on the third floor always had my shit flossy. I had all the designs and patterns in my cornrows. She had my hair grown down to my ass by the time I hit fourth grade. You couldn't tell me nothing. I knew I was the cutest chick on Fifty-fifth Drive.

I wished I had a mom who was more compassionate though. She basically gave me the necessities. I had to figure the rest of that shit out on my own. When I woke up for school most mornings, she was just getting in from a long night out, or already passed out on the couch. However, she always made sure my lunch was packed, and I always had a few dollars to grab something to eat on the way to school. That was my mom's love language. She never told me she loved me. Probably because she never heard it from her mom. But she always made sure I had the best of the best. That was how I knew she fucked with me the hard way. She very well could have left me hungry and raggedy as fuck. I would have just blended in with the rest of these raggedy fucks out here.

When I met Skye, Selah, and Sajdah, I hit the jackpot. They were some of the nicest girls I ever met. Well, Selah and Skye were. I didn't know what the fuck Sajdah's beef was, and I wasn't about to be losing sleep trying to figure it out. One thing my momma always told me: if a bitch don't like you, fuck that ho.

"Don't you be sweatin' no bitches, you hear me? There's too many hoes out here for you to waste your time on one. Make another damn friend or none at all. You can't trust these hoes anyway."

I always lived by those words. My mother had never given me bad advice. A lot of gems dropped from that one. She was a real G, and because of everything she'd taught me and everything I'd seen her do, how she moved in her circle, you got who I was now: a ruthless bitch who loved hard for those she let in but wasn't afraid to make moves that were beneficial to me exclusively. I was taught that, no matter what, look out for numero uno. Trust and believe no one else would.

I tried to be sensitive to Selah's situation, but I could only have but so much compassion for her. She wasn't supposed to pull the trigger, but she did, and now she had to deal with it. I'd been riding with and for her since day one. Those lopsided friendships catch you off guard every time.

Sigh. I decided it was time to take my ass in the house before I started getting all emotional and shit. I missed my fucking friends, and I didn't even have some good dick to take my mind off it for the night. As I gathered my things, I was startled by Chase's phone ringing. I picked it up slowly and held it as it buzzed in my hand. The name Goon was on the screen. I didn't know whether to answer the shit. What the hell would I say? What if he had used the Find My iPhone tracker and now some crazy asses were on the way to get me? I almost shit on myself just thinking of what would happen to me. Instead of denying the call, I let it ring out. I didn't want him to know that someone definitely had the phone. Just as I was trying to turn it off, a text came through from Goon. I started shaking all over again.

I know that someone else has Chase's phone. Please answer so we can talk. I won't hurt you. I promise.

I left that shit on read as I powered the phone off and gathered my stuff to get in the crib real quick in case they had the drop on me. I wasn't dying tonight over some dead dick that wasn't mine to begin with. By the time I got inside I was out of breath and still shaking. I had to sit down and think. This didn't have to be a bad thing. I just had to figure out how I was going to play this shit out to my benefit. A slow smile crept across my face as I began to think of what I would do next. I'd see how Monday at the bank played out, but something was telling me I may have just gotten the help I'd been praying for.

Chapter 6

Goon

Time to Backtrack

My boy was definitely a done bun. I hadn't heard from him in months, and that was not his style. We spoke at least three times a week every week, and he always came down for the playoffs. After speaking with a few guys from the crew, I knew some bullshit had transpired. Although we had things handled, I needed to know what the fuck happened. I was out of the drug game, but I knew they looked up to me because I was there since our college days. I wasn't about to jump back in, but I wasn't about to leave them hanging either. My gun still shot the same as before, bullets still fully stocked. The NBA changed me, but I was still deeply rooted in the streets.

Things stayed low-key surprisingly, but I knew it wouldn't last long. We had to restore order to keep a tight ship the way Chase would have wanted it. You already know the minute fools know a link in the chain is broken, they think the entire fence is down. We had to especially make sure shit was good before the locals started trying to make moves or some nut ass right in this crew decided to be froggy. We had to watch the streets, but we had to watch the clique closer than ever before.

When I got the call that Chase was missing, I was floored. We had just won a game against our biggest rival, and I was on a high like you wouldn't believe. To beat them in their own house was a slap in the face, and we were really feeling ourselves after the game was over. Before the game I briefly wondered why I hadn't heard from Chase. By now he would have already been making plans to crash at the crib. I made a mental note to call him later in the evening once the game was over. Too bad I was too late.

By the time we got down to his crib, it was squeaky clean in that motherfucker, and there was no sign in sight of the bitch he said was living there. My first thought was to check the security cameras, but that shit was already dismantled, and I didn't have any access to cloud storage for him. I didn't know if he was the only one gone or if both they asses got got. She didn't have a damn thing left in the crib. Hell, even the dog's shit was gone. Not too long ago she was in the process of building a walk-in closet, so what happened? Too many unanswered questions had me frustrated and ready for war, but with who?

There weren't any drugs in the crib, so his story wouldn't have made the news. Cops were only interested in dead black men if there were drugs involved. They were always looking for the next big bust. This dude was wiped out of any money he had in the crib, and as a rule, ever since we witnessed his brother's death, we never kept product on the premises. That was what the trap houses were for. However, I did take note that there was another death around the time of his disappearance. Sis was on the news grieving her sister after she was found in a trunk in the projects or some shit. I never met sis in person, but I believe that was the girl he was trying to wife up. I didn't know she had an identical twin sister though. So which bitch was his? The live one or the dead one? No one in the crew knew either, even though they had helped her in the crib with some shit a few times. I really couldn't fault them for that though. It wasn't their job to know. Chase was just like me. He kept his girl out of business that wasn't hers. That way no one would have a connection to him through her. I felt it. He did the right thing, just at the wrong damn time.

Those hoes were identical down to the damn bone, and I was sure only they momma could tell them apart. Some dumb shit done transpired, and I refused to let it rest until I got some answers. How in the fuck was the entire crew clueless? Whoever did this was excellent at what they did and covered their tracks down to the smallest detail. No one had a lead, but that wouldn't stop me. Somebody saw something, trust and believe. I just had to find out who it was. Whether you believe it or not, there's always a watchful eye on everything we do. I hadn't had a good night's sleep since he'd been gone, and I refused to until I got what I needed.

Some greedy-ass person definitely got to him. No money left? I was sure he had something in here. It wasn't enough to take a big loss if things got crazy, but just enough to stay off the cameras at the bank. This shit wasn't sitting right in my spirit, and I needed to know what the hell was going on. Things just weren't adding up. This man never got caught slipping, so what happened this time? He mentioned having a bank account before, but where? Was the money still there? Did the bitch take it? Lord, this was just too much!

This was what I knew: a little over a year ago he finally bagged this bad bitch he kept mentioning. He tried to get her to come out with him to meet me, but due to the schedule at the gig, she couldn't make it. One day we spoke about it just being a thought, and then the ho had moved in by the time we spoke again. He told me she ran with a few chicks who were bad too, but she was the baddest one. One of the girls was her sister. This dumb ass never said she was an identical twin sister, just that she was on dime status also. That was information folks needed to know in case some shit like this happened.

When he came out to see me, he was dead set on marrying this chick. I mean, he was really ready to turn in his player card and shit. Any chick who had him ready to pack it up was my kind of girl, and I was genuinely happy for him. I didn't think Chase would ever settle down with just one woman. I had been telling this fool for years to get out of the game. Shit, she was telling him the same shit I was telling him: take all the fucking money you been stacking and open up a few stores. He knew how to manage a team, so it wasn't like he would have to physically man the stores. I even told him I would invest in the dream. I wanted him to come be my manager, but he couldn't let the streets go.

"Man, this ball shit is your dream, Goon. That's why I can't let you get in too deep. I need you to do better for both of us," he said to me when I finally got drafted officially and asked him to come along. That just made me respect him even more, and I genuinely loved him like a brother, same mother different father.

So let's get these businesses popping. Hire a manager and a crew and make this fucking bread. Homegirl had him ready to do the right thing. Only thing about that is you don't just "get out" of the game. There are some loose ends and some shit you have to move around before you dip on 'em. You have to make sure everything you've built is capable of standing after you're gone. All of this shit is like a house of cards. If that foundation ain't stable, that shit for sure will come tumbling down. And just like with any card game, you know the queen and the king run the deck, but it's always a joker that will try you every time. Save that big joker for last, and just when they think they won with the last ace in their hand, boom! Sweep the fucking board!

Last time he was in town we had a blast. He scouted a few club locations while he was here because he was thinking about venturing into owning a few nightclubs, and we all know Miami is the place to be for that nightlife vibe. He even spoke to some guys on the team who had some insight into the business he was trying to get into. It really seemed like he had all of his shit lined up and was ready to start moving forward. Had I known the last time I saw him would be the last time I'd see him, I would have hugged him a little longer. He was the reason I was here. When we met in college, I really had only the basics, but this man put me on and refused to let me fuck up my dreams of going to the NBA. I had the entire hood riding on my back, and he always made sure we were straight. I owed him my life, and I needed to find out who took his.

I didn't really expect anyone to answer his phone. Every so often, when he popped up in my mind, I'd send a random text to his number just to see what would happen. For a while I got nothing. Even when I got to Philly and searched for his phone, I never got a ping back, and after all this time I was surprised that the shit was even still on. What did this fool do? Pay his bill up for three years or some shit? That didn't stop me from calling and texting though. This shit just wasn't like him, and I felt like he wanted me to find out the truth.

As time went on, I noticed that when I would look back at previous texts they began showing up as read, as opposed to just staying delivered. This brought up the question again. Was the dead bitch his bitch, or the live one? Did she have his phone? Did someone in the crew do this shit to him, and they had his phone? That little action gave me a little bit of hope that finally I would get some information. So I made the decision that I would not stop calling and texting until someone answered.

Today I was just chilling thinking about my friend. Shantel sent me a pic of the baby earlier in the day, and I couldn't get over how much he looked like Chase. He looked more like Chase than his own dad, and it made me wonder if Chase had ever hit that shit. Just thinking that this child would never know his dad or his uncle just caused unrest in my spirit, and I decided to call the phone to see what happened. It was a sunny Saturday afternoon. Maybe today was the day.

When I dialed the phone, to my surprise, it actually began to ring. That shit caught me off guard, and I held my breath the entire time hoping someone would answer. When they didn't, I immediately sent a text letting them know that I knew they had Chase's phone and I just wanted to talk. The message sat on read. When I texted again a few minutes later, it just said delivered, which meant the phone was turned off. I was ready to hop on a private jet and get to Philly ASAP, but I had to sit down and gather my thoughts. My suspicion was confirmed, but I couldn't be sloppy with this shit. I had to make sure this played out just right. Whoever had his phone was about to be mad as shit that they were about to die.

"Baby, you hungry?" my fiancé asked as she sauntered in from the kitchen in a sports bra and boy shorts in my team colors. I went back to the hood and got her. She had been riding with me since middle school, and even when I left to go to college, she kept it tight and right for me. Even after I told her to go ahead and start dating because I didn't know what would come of this school thing.

I didn't ask anyone to keep an eye on her, but every cat in the hood who tried to holler was quickly shut down, and it was reported to me that she never let a soul touch her. That was how I knew she was a keeper, and it killed me that Chase never got to meet her. When he came out, she was off visiting family. We kept mostly late-night conversations, so she was asleep most of the times he called. He was supposed to be the best man in my wedding, and I in his. Who took our dream away?

Preparing a quick text to Demon, the next in line in the crew, I knew it was time for me to get back to Philly and do some digging, even if I had to bring my own damn shovel. I was not about to leave until I got something solid. I told him not to tell anyone I was coming. I needed to see these dudes in their natural habitat, just to see who was moving funny. The season was just about over, so I would have nothing but time to look for my boy.

"I'll take a small plate, babe," I responded, not wanting her hot meal to go to waste. Her grandma taught her how to cook, and she was serious with those pots in the kitchen. While she went to make my plate, I called my grandmother up to let her know I would be in town, and to keep that a secret from the family also. At times like this I needed to be surrounded by my family, but I didn't feel like all the begging and fake shit. Cousins who never liked me, all of a sudden, were my biggest fans. *Skip past me with that dumb-ass shit. I ain't got nothing for you!* I needed some of those prayer-circle prayers from the mothers of the church. You know those sanctified prayers hit different from those closer to God.

After my meal, I gave baby girl what she wanted, making sure her knees touched her ears while I went deep, just the way she liked it. The minute I made her my wife I was going to put a baby in her. She would have a boy, and he would be named after his uncle Chase. I rocked her ass to sleep like Buns did to Keisha in *Belly*. Unfortunately, sleep wouldn't come easy for me, and I found myself staring at the ceiling for hours after she was knocked out for the night. The last thing I remembered before finally succumbing to the sandman was asking Chase to give me a sign, anything, so that he could finally rest in peace.

Chapter 7

Selah

Goodbye and Good Riddance

"I did this for you. He really wanted me, but I knew I wouldn't have time for him."

Boom! The bullet flew across the room, and just before it connected and splattered my sister's brain out of the back of her head, I woke up in a cold sweat. The tears wasted no time spilling from my tightly closed eyes, and my heart kept time with a marathon runner in my chest. I felt like I was going to vomit but didn't have the energy to get up and run to the bathroom, so I swallowed my fear back down. Every night since my sister had been gone it'd been like this. I was lonely, afraid, guilty, but I deserved all of this hell I was living in, so I laid my ass back down and concentrated on slowing my breathing until it returned to normal. Eventually I would fall back to sleep, and before I could get any real rest, it would be morning.

What if things had gone differently though? I killed myself with the what-if's more than anything else. If you've ever lost someone close to you, you know exactly what I mean. Multiply that feeling by a million if it was your fault they died. I wasn't the only one out here in these streets trying to keep it together. There were some other guilty bitches losing sleep just like my ass was. I knew that for a fact.

I rolled over and tried to get comfortable as I thought about what was on my plate for the day. My therapy appointment was at 11:00 a.m. I would be taking my lunch early, and I was happy about it. The look of sorrow everyone had for me when I showed up at work was suffocating. Cici held me so tight every morning, and I just wanted it to stop. She often mentioned how she couldn't imagine living without her sister. *Shit, try being the one who killed her ass, and it changes the game drastically.* I wanted to say those exact words to her but never did.

You'll want to kill yourself every waking moment of every day that you're still alive, but you won't because that's some coward-ass shit. You'll just continue to avoid eye contact because the eyes tell everything. You will cry every night until you finally fall asleep and the night terrors wake you again. You will get up exhausted and ready to call it quits, but you will eat that shit and take care of the

ones who are left because you're the reason behind
the pain. And just when you finally get to sleep, the
smell of breakfast wakes you up.

I opened one eye and then the other, trying to get
myself fully awake. The smell of cinnamon, peaches,
and cream wafted through my room and wrapped me
in a hug. My stomach growled in protest as a small
smile struggled to curve my lips. My dad was making peach-cobbler pancakes. Messing with my parents, I'd be a million pounds soon, but those pancakes were not going to be passed up.

Hopping out of bed, I mustered up what little
energy I had to get myself together. As I went out
to the hall, I put my hand on my sister's bedroom
door to feel her energy. She still had such a heavy
presence in this house. I didn't linger in the shower
this morning like I usually did. I still had to call my
accountant to have him draw up papers for Vice later.
Just thinking of her name made my head hurt. She
was hiding something, but what? As soon as I could
get my ducks in a row, I was going to figure it out.

By the time I made it downstairs, my dad was at
the table reading the paper on his tablet, and my
mom was across from him, looking through various
furniture catalogs, her food barely touched. She
had yet to regain her full appetite, and every time I
saw her, she looked more fragile than the last time.
She felt like skin and bones when I hugged her. I
wanted to apologize for the hurt, but she wouldn't

understand why. Where she was once kind of plump with flawless skin, now she just looked skeletal and ashy, and I could see her hair was starting to fall out, probably from a lack of protein. It was heartbreaking.

"Good morning, Ma," I greeted her as I planted a soft kiss on her cheek.

"How do you feel about this chair?" she responded, pointing at an overpriced office chair that I assumed was for her space she was creating in the basement.

"I think you can find that cheaper, Ma. Good morning, Daddy." I gave my dad a quick kiss on the cheek and held on to him a little longer. It had to be horrible watching your wife deteriorate right in front of you. I was already feeling smothered and started packing my breakfast to go.

"I will be in a little late today. I have some business I need to take care of." I spoke more to my daddy. I knew my mom was in her own little world and paying me no mind.

"Okay, baby. Be safe."

Giving my parents one last kiss, I made my way out the door to work. There were a lot of people out when I arrived at the train, which meant it was running behind. I was in no rush to get to the office anyway, so I found myself a little corner and began enjoying my breakfast in the corner. I just wanted a little sample of what was to come.

You ever feel like someone was staring at you? Across the platform was a guy who looked like someone I might have known, but I wasn't so sure. I really couldn't see him good and thought maybe I was just overreacting. There were a lot of people standing near me, so he could have been looking at anyone. Taking a look at my surroundings, I saw a few cuties on their way to work this morning. He definitely could have been eyeballing anyone. His look was so intense though. Not inviting in the least.

As my train pulled up, I moved closer to the edge of the platform, quickly contemplating jumping in front of it but deciding not to mess up the morning for all these people because I had demons I wasn't ready to deal with yet. Once aboard, I made sure to get to a window so that I could see the guy. We made eye contact again. As the train pulled off, he held up his hand like a gun and took a shot at me. The imaginary bullet landed in my chest and caused me to lose my breath briefly.

By the time I got to work I was completely frazzled, and I hid myself in the private employee bathroom to get myself together. Who the fuck was that? Were Chase's people looking for me? Did I imagine all of that happening? I was slowly starting to unravel, and I knew it was because I didn't exactly have all the answers. I didn't want to worry my parents, so I couldn't call them. I didn't trust Vice, and Skye would listen, but she had her own shit going on. Picking up the phone, I called the next best person on the list—my therapist.

"Is it possible to move my appointment up? I feel like I'm going into crisis mode," I spoke into my phone, barely able to hold my tears in.

"I'm sure I can move some things around. Are you in a safe place?" my therapist asked. He reminded me so much of Chase it was scary but soothing at the same time.

"Yes, I'm at work."

"Okay, I can see you at nine. Head on over. I'll move some things around in the meantime."

I thanked him at least ten times before hanging up the phone. My next call was to FMLA to let them know I was taking a day. Every time I thought I was going to be okay, something crazy happened and ruined my entire day.

My therapist's office was right in Rittenhouse Square, not far from where I worked, so it wouldn't take me long to get there. Scouting my surroundings to make sure old spooky wasn't following me, I gave my breakfast to a homeless person on the corner as I made my way to the train station. Then I decided against it and hid back in the building until my Uber showed up.

So many thoughts ran through my mind. What would I tell him? I needed some of this guilt off, and I needed it off ASAP.

When the car pulled up to his office building, I looked around to see who was outside before getting out, and I made a quick dash to the building door before anyone could shoot at me. My heart was beating so fast it was surprising I hadn't stroked out yet. I scratched my name in the guest book and made my way up to the penthouse. He gave us a code that only belonged to us and only worked during the time of our appointment. This meant that he really did some quick work to squeeze me in, and I wanted to make it worth his while. Before I could blink, I was ushered back to his office, where he was waiting for me.

I lost all track of time when I made eye contact with him. He reminded me so much of the person I ideally would have married had I not killed him. He was a shade or two lighter, but he definitely had that look. For weeks before ever coming to see him, I stared at his picture in the catalog I received from my insurance company. It was a toss-up between him and this lady, but I quickly decided that I didn't want to speak to a female. They hadn't been proving themselves trustworthy lately. Although I knew she had to keep my info confidential, it would be just my damn luck she'd know somebody who knew somebody I knew, and I just couldn't chance it.

I felt a sense of calm come over me as soon as I sat across from him. He just had this relaxed vibe about him that was contagious. Like I could tell him anything in the world and have no worries. I mean, yeah, that was his job to make me feel secure, but he did it without effort. Choosing him was the best decision I'd made lately.

"Tell me what's on your mind," he started after he got his notepad out and started his recorder. For some reason I was always intimidated by the recorder, even though he assured me he was the only one who listened to the playbacks.

"You ever have a secret so big that you want to tell someone but can't?"

"For sure. Those are the ones I pray about the most," he responded. "Why do you feel you can't share it?"

"Because if I do, I'll end up in jail," I responded with a straight face. I was sure he thought I was being dramatic, but the truth would not set this bird free. It would land me caged right in the fucking slammer.

"I'm not saying you have to tell the authorities," he said with a slight chuckle that sounded sexy as hell to me. "But you can confide in someone. I usually leave religion out of therapy, but how strong is your faith? Even if you tell no one else but God, you said it out loud and you can now move forward. God can't put you in jail, as you mentioned."

But God can put me in the hellfire. Sheesh, this shit was getting harder than I wanted it to. Maybe he had a point. I knew something had to be done to move forward, and I decided that after I did everything I needed to do today, tomorrow I would start to heal . . . or maybe the next day. *Sigh.* It was just so frustrating.

We spoke a little more about my mom and how things were going at home. I didn't even get into the guy at the train station, which was the thing that triggered these feelings in the first place. I actually felt silly now and decided to just let it pass for now. If it happened again, then I would bring it up.

I thanked him for his time and rescheduled with the receptionist once I got back up front. There was something about this chick that I just couldn't put my finger on, but I chalked it up to paranoia. I wished I could have taken her pic on the low to show Skye, but I just let it go. I would definitely be praying for clarity this evening, but shit was just getting too crazy for me lately.

Still erring on the side of caution, just in case I wasn't tripping, I waited inside the lobby until my Uber pulled up, making a mad dash for the door once I got outside. When I got back home, I called and had the paperwork drawn up and the check printed so that I could be ready for Vice later. I started to just have her meet me earlier, but I didn't want her to know I wasn't at work today. She could have had dude following me for all I knew. I didn't put anything past her.

As time got closer to meet her, I started getting nervous for some reason. What if I had to knock this bitch in her face at the bank? From what I got from Skye, she clearly felt like she deserved more than what I had given her thus far, and maybe she did. At the same time, my gut kept telling me that she ain't as squeaky clean as she was trying to appear. Let her tell it, she saved me from my evil twin sister who, as time went on, wasn't nearly as evil as portrayed. Glancing at the collection of disks from Chase's place, I knew it was time for me to go ahead and see what was on them. Whatever truth was on there had to see the light of day whether I wanted it to or not.

I'll be at the bank at 3:00 p.m. Meet me inside and bring identification.

I shot a text over to Vice with instructions for this afternoon. At first I was just going to give her a couple hundred thousand, but I knew Vice. If I didn't give her more, she'd be back. On some real shit, no price would be enough for her, but that was where the contract came in. Once I gave her this money, that was it, and contractually I wouldn't owe her anything else. I may have changed the amount at least six times before I settled on giving her a flat $2 million. It was slightly more than what I gave Skye, considering she already got a lump sum that she blew through, but it would definitely be more than she was expecting to get. I mean, what was she going to do? Take me to court and tell the judge I wouldn't split money from my drug dealer boyfriend she helped me bury? *Girl, bye.*

Setting my alarm, I lay down for a quick nap before meeting up with her. That entire ordeal this morning took everything I had left, and all I could do was cry. Damn, I missed my sister and Chase's dumb ass. The only thing keeping me from joining them on the other side was that I knew my parents couldn't take another blow to the gut like that. Taking my phone out, I scrolled through my contacts and pulled up Chase. A few times I'd received a text from his number, and I wondered who had his phone. Before I could stop myself, I tapped the phone icon and dialed his number. It rang once and picked up, but I couldn't really make out the sounds in the background. It was like the phone was in a bag or someone's back pocket. I listened for a minute more and then just hung up. I didn't need whoever it was who had his phone coming for me.

As I lay on the bed quietly, it sounded like the damn videotapes were calling me. Well, they were actually a collection of DVDs that he had set up in this system. I had the entire system sitting next to my dresser on the floor. Before I could talk myself out of it, I jumped up and connected it to my TV. It didn't take long to get set up at all, and I made sure my bedroom door was locked before starting the video.

Seeing Chase alive and well sent a shock through my system that I wasn't ready for. Just watching him walk and talk sent me into a crying fit that I couldn't control. I was literally only a few minutes into the first video, but I had to turn it off. I wasn't ready, and I wasn't going to force myself, even though I knew if

I wanted the truth, I'd have to suck it up and get the info that was right in front of me . . . just not today.

Lying down, I closed my eyes and eventually fell asleep, being awakened by the alarm a short time later. I got up, refreshed my face, and headed over to the bank to meet Vice. I just hoped that she would be civilized. I was really down to my very last nerve, and I was not prepared to battle with her today. Saying a quick prayer, I made my way across town. If I timed this right, this entire ordeal could be over in less than five minutes.

Chapter 8

Vice

Who Wants to Be a Millionaire?

I sat in my car fucking up a chicken box from Popeye's while I waited for Selah to pull up. I really hoped I wouldn't have to dog walk this ho today. I was down to my last few dollars from that bullshit stack she gave me the other day, and I really needed her to show up. Shit, I'd been hungry all weekend. Not that she'd ever let me down in the past, but death changes a person. We were not the people we used to be. I was close to having to return one of my bags if she didn't come through today. Bills were due, and I was not in the mood to fuck for money right now. I shouldn't have to, considering there was still money on deck that I felt I should have access to. I showed up an entire hour early so that she couldn't say shit about me being late. I wasn't giving her any excuse to shine brighter than she already was.

I saw that she called Chase's phone. What the hell was that about? Was she hoping he answered or some shit? Wanted to hear her ex's voice one more time? I heard the phone buzz in my bag and was caught off guard because I thought I had turned the shit off and that the guy was calling back. When I saw her name, I clicked the ANSWER button, but I didn't say shit just to see what she would do. She hung up without saying a word. I immediately turned the phone off afterward. I wondered if she knew I had the phone and was just testing me. I quickly dismissed the thought, because if she knew, she would have definitely come for me by now. There was no questioning that fact. Above all else, Selah loved Chase, and she probably still couldn't believe she was the reason he was gone.

Speaking of dude, who was he exactly? Clearly, he was some kind of connection to Chase, but how? Brother? Cousin? Squad? Selah never really told us much about his background, which made me wonder how much her slow ass knew. We could have been dealing with some real live monsters here. How far would he go to track down Chase's killer? I knew I needed to give him a call, but what would I say? "Hi, my name is Vice, and I set your boy up to be killed because I thought he was cheating on my homegirl"? He'd have the entire hood on me for sure, and I already knew I couldn't handle that kind of heat. Too many people knew where to find me, and I could definitely be touched. I had to find a way to flip this shit on Selah so that she'd be the target. Only thing was if she died, there was no way to get the money. I wasn't her damn twin. I couldn't just switch my ass up in the bank and make transactions like she did. I just knew that, if nothing else, I needed to get more than what she was willing to give. I'd figure out how later on.

Finishing off my box, I cleaned up just in time to see Selah enter the branch. I didn't want to seem all thirsty, considering she was a few minutes early herself, but in reality, I was parched! The first thing I was going to do was get me a good meal after I got this money. Maggiano's would definitely get some coins if I headed to KOP. If not, Center City was on the list. I had so many options from Ruth's Chris to Fogo de Chão, I didn't even know where to start. Hell, maybe I'd rent out Buca di Beppo and treat the hood to a meal they probably could never afford otherwise. I was pretty sure I was about to be living high off the hog, and as always, I showed the hood love.

As my mind began to wander on all the options I would soon have, I came to a quick realization—I didn't know how much this bitch was giving me. I could very well walk out with $500. *Nah, Selah wouldn't be doing all this for that little bit of money. A contract is not needed for 500 stank-ass dollars, or is it?* Just as my anxiety was starting to get the best of me, my phone buzzed. Snatching it from the passenger seat, I saw a message from Selah letting me know she was at the bank.

I'm here.

Okay, just pulled up, I lied as I gathered my belongings to go inside, spritzing my body once more to get the smell of chicken off of me. I left Chase's phone in the car just in case this was a setup. I didn't know why I was so nervous all of a sudden. The butterflies in my stomach had me feeling so nauseated. I felt lightheaded as I got to the door and had to lean on the building to get my shit together before walking inside. I was not about to fuck around and pass out, missing out on this coin.

As I approached her, my legs felt like wet noodles, not one ounce of support in them shits. I tried to shake it off, but Selah had me in my bag. *Straighten up, bitch,* my alter ego warned me as I adjusted my bag in the crook of my arm. Of course, I was Gucci down to the pumps, looking model fresh in this bitch. She was not about to think I was slipping in these streets. She wanted to know what I spent my money on? Now was the best time to show her.

When I got past the security door, I saw her sitting at one of the tables chatting with two guys. I was sure the one behind the desk was the banker, but who was that next to her? My anxiety quickly turned to anger as I got closer to the table.

"Here she is," she replied with a fake smile. Everyone stood up to greet me, and I was offered a chair to sit in.

"Hello, everyone," I responded, trying to sound like I had some sense about me. Now was not the time for hood shit. I may have been from the gutter, but I learned a lot of shit being at the bottom of the totem pole.

"So as discussed . . ." Selah began, sliding over a small stack of papers. She didn't waste any time getting to the point. You would never think we were friends once. "I have a one-time payment for you upon signing this contract. This is Joe, my lawyer. He is here to answer any questions you may have before signing. Chad can help you with opening an account if you'd like, or he can cash the check out for you to do with what you want today."

I took the papers she slid over, resisting the urge to smack her across the damn face with them. I didn't want to hate her, but she was making it so easy. Skimming through the papers to read the parts I could understand, I saw that she was cutting me a check for $2 million. I almost started twerking in my seat when I saw the amount. Oh, she showed the hell out! I quickly skimmed through the rest of the document so I could get this check before she changed her mind.

"Okay, you have a pen?" I asked the banker.

"Please keep in mind that once this check is cashed, you are not to contact my client for any more monetary contributions." Her lawyer spit out some legal mumbo jumbo that I completely ignored. If things went the way they were brewing in my head, I'd have the money I needed from her plus some.

"Okay, got it. No problem," I replied as I scribbled some form of my signature on the bottom of the check. I was thinking it wouldn't matter what name I signed if I denied it later, but then I realized Selah was smarter than the average bear. If push came to shove, all they would have to do was pull the surveillance from today to show in court. Yeah, I'd definitely have to get her a different way.

"Congrats on the come-up!" the bank teller chimed in all hype. I just looked at him like he had three heads. He barely noticed. "How do you want to cash out? Are you depositing your funds, or do you want cash?"

"Actually, I haven't decided yet. Can I bring the check back before closing?" I asked, not wanting to appear desperate about having the money. I guessed I was trying to show Selah that I didn't need her money. That maybe I wanted her friendship more. Sike, who the hell was I trying to fool? I just didn't want this ho to know where I banked at. The minute we were done here, I'd be driving my ass down to PFCU to get this money set up right.

"Sure! We are here until six p.m., but with a check in this amount you may want to get here at five."

"Okay, no problem. I'll see you soon."

We all gathered our stuff and prepared to walk out. I noticed Selah and her lawyer lagged behind a little to have a private conversation, but I really didn't give a fuck. I'd take the $2 million for now and figure out how to get more later.

As I made my way to my car, I decided that today would be the day to set my plan in motion. *I mean, why not?* She still wasn't playing fair with this bread, so I guessed I had to just take what was owed to me. I sat in my car to gather my thoughts. *Do I take the check to my bank and wait for them to clear it? That could take days, and I'm hungry today. Or do I just go in here and cash out so that I can take actual cash to my bank? Like, bitch, I'm officially a millionaire! Who'da thunk it?* I was so fucking happy but so sad at the same time. Money is truly the root of all evil. It will break up a family and a friendship every single damn time.

Deciding on the obviously right thing to do, I got back out of the car to go inside. Just as I was crossing to open the door, Selah came out. We made eye contact that felt awkward. I started to just keep pushing past her ass, but I needed her to think we were on the same page kind of. She looked like the last place she wanted to be in the world was outside.

"So you're all taken care of, right?" she asked, looking around nervously like she was afraid.

"Monetarily I'm good, but what happened to us, sis?" I asked, trying to sound sincere. I was actually so far removed from the friendship it wasn't even funny. I worked up a few tears and everything. I definitely could have been an actress. She, on the other hand, looked preoccupied.

"I'm not sure, but when you have time, we can discuss it. I need to get going," she said, practically running off to her car.

I looked around to see if anything looked out of the ordinary, and all I saw was the hustle and bustle of shoppers at Penrose Plaza. I knew enough to know that things aren't always what they seem, though, and I could very well have eyes on me as well.

Just as paranoia kicked in, I dipped into the bank to make the transaction, deciding to take $10,000 in large bills, depositing half the balance into an account, and taking a cashier's check to PFCU so that I didn't have to transport all that money.

Once I was done, I called Ruth's Chris for takeout, put some gas in my tank, because Lord knows I was riding on fumes, and took my ass straight the hell home. Grabbing Chase's phone off the charger, I powered it on and stared at it for what felt like ages. Looking through the call log, I redialed the number that matched the name of Goon. I was scared to dial, but in reality, he needed me. Or so I convinced myself as I listened to the phone ring on the other end. I didn't know what I was going to say to him or if he was even going to answer. Where did this guy live? The number wasn't local, but nowadays that didn't really mean much.

"Speak your piece," a groggy but deep voice answered the phone. My voice was stuck in my throat, and I couldn't get a word out. "You called back, so you must have something to say," the guy I assumed was Goon spoke.

"Yes, I have some information for you, but I can't give it to you right now. I'll be calling you in a few days from another phone. If you're smart, you'll answer it."

Click.

My heart was beating so fucking fast as I powered the phone down completely just in case he tried to call. Once I got my breathing back together, I went ahead and ate my dinner while I waited for my young buck to get here. I decided I would go get one of those Cricket phones to communicate with him. I figured as long as it wasn't an iPhone, they wouldn't be able to find me as easily. Shit, if I played this right, I might be able to dig in his pockets, too! The more I thought about this, the more things started to become clearer. I had to slow walk this one so that I'd be the last man standing.

Chapter 9

Goon

In Search of the Truth

Now my ass was up. I had just gotten to sleep after putting my girl down for the night. We got a bun in the oven, and her hormones had her on fire! We weren't planning on it to happen this soon. I definitely wanted to marry her first, but my pull-out game was weak sauce, and I guessed those pills she was taking weren't strong enough. Sincc the season was over, it was like free reign in this bitch. She took the liberty of climbing and sucking all over me whenever she felt like it. During the game season, sex was limited because Coach wanted us on our A game. You'd be surprised how a nut can ruin your stamina. We would go for months at a time without it, and with a woman as fine as mine it was hard to stay off of her. A nut could definitely drain you, and we refused to risk the championship. I loved that she was understanding, oftentimes not even accepting me just giving her head to hold her over.

"I want the entire experience, daddy. I can wait," she'd whisper in my ear. That shit just turned me on even more. When I finally did get it, I made sure to make up for all that lost time. If it were up to me, she would never leave the bed. That was part of the reason that, while I was on the road, none of those other women interested me. I knew what I had at home could never be replaced. She was down for anything I wanted to try, short of a threesome. I wasn't interested, and I would never disrespect my lady like that. That was really some baldhead-ho shit that I was just not trying to be a part of.

I'd always wanted kids, but I was afraid. Would I even be a good father? Ain't like I had an example of how this shit was supposed to go. Not that he was a deadbeat. Some other deadbeat took him from us before I could get to know him. Drugs snatched my mom from me, so all I had left was Gram. How would I provide for someone else when I couldn't provide for myself? I knew how rough my people had it raising me, and I just couldn't bring myself to transfer those same feelings to the next generation. My mom barely ate most nights, but she always made sure we were good up until she couldn't. The streets played dirty, and I didn't want anything coming from me being lost in the struggle.

My girl had been with me since day one. Even when they teased me back in the day. She saw in me what I couldn't see in myself, and that was why, when I made it, I went back to the hood and got her. Aside from Chase, she was the only friend I had in the world. Them two and my church family. That was why this was so hard. God said, "Thou shalt not kill," and "Vengeance is mine," but I just couldn't sit back and let Him take His time with this karma. I needed to make moves, and hopefully I could pray this sin away when I was done handling my business. I needed to see this get-back happen with my own eyes, and I would not stop until it was done.

When the phone buzzed, I sat up instantly. I literally just got some lunchtime pussy and was enjoying my nap. Luckily the phone didn't wake up my angel. When she wasn't trying to suck the skin off my dick, she was feeling nauseated and sleepy, and I didn't like to bother her. When I saw Chase's name flash up on the screen, I answered as quickly as I could before whoever had his phone hung up.

I was super surprised to hear a female's voice. Who in the hell was this bitch, and how was she connected to my brother? She was a bold one for sure, but I was sure she had some information I needed, so I stayed neutral. Clearly, she had no clue who she was dealing with and the level of danger she was now in. Or if she did know, she didn't care and thought she had a win. I had so many questions, but she didn't really give me enough time to ask her anything. She said she would call me back in a few days, and I guessed I'd just have to wait until then. I'd be flying out to Philly this coming weekend, and I wanted to have as much info in place as possible before the hunt began. She was a courageous one, but she would definitely regret fucking with me. I was not so far removed from the streets that I couldn't find her. I just needed a few more clues.

I didn't want to upset my lady, so I didn't say anything to her about this. I didn't want her stressed out and to risk her miscarrying. She knew I was hurting over Chase's disappearance, but I really didn't talk much about it. It was embedded in me from a young'un not to really show emotions. People will use what you told them against you every single time, and I refused to let any of the scabs have one up on me. We didn't discuss our problems in the hood. We just tried our best to make it through each day. My lady knew what she knew about me because she was in the struggle too. She knew what it was like to miss a meal, having to take care of younger siblings, and going without so they could have. Wc were cut from the same cloth and saved each other when we least expected it.

She didn't need this kind of stress on her, with her being pregnant. She was always a nervous wreck every time I left anyway, so I didn't want to put any- thing extra on her. As far as she was concerned, I was going to Philly to check in on my grandma, and that wasn't a complete lie. I'd definitely have to check in on my first love while I was there, but I also had to look into these unsolved mysteries surrounding my boy. She couldn't travel with me this time because the semester had just started for her, and she didn't want to miss any classes. That, and the morning sickness had her down for the count, and she didn't want to chance being sick on the plane ride over.

A part of me wanted to rent a jet and head over there immediately, but I needed to think this through. Moving fast never got anyone anywhere quicker. You always have to backtrack. We already lost enough time with this situation, and when I got whoever did this to my boy, I needed to make sure it was the right person and that they got everything they deserved.

The eagle will be landing at 1500 in about 48.

I sent the text out to Demon to expect me in a few days. He was doing good holding down the crew, but last we talked, we figured we might have to put a few in the ground sooner rather than later. I knew someone would act a fool since Chase was gone. There's always one who wants to test you. Always remember there is no loyalty among thieves and killers. He had it all under control though, and once I got there, any pressing issues would be handled. It'd been a while since I had to get my hands dirty, and Demon wasn't exactly gung ho about me even getting involved.

"Dog, you made it out. Something the rest of us probably will never do. We got it. You just keep dribbling that ball."

"I hear you," I replied as we sat and sipped a few beers. He had a blunt in rotation, but the NBA tested for drugs, and I didn't want to jeopardize my shit. *"But for my brother, I wouldn't have it any other way. He'd burn the town down trying to find my killer. It's only right I do the same."*

He knew the love Chase and I had for each other and quickly realized there was no need trying to convince me to do anything other than what I set out to get done. If it was the last thing I did on earth, I was going to find out who killed my brother.

Chapter 10

Vice

Plan A

"Bitch, I definitely got the fucking job," my home-girl Renee screamed into my ear. I didn't even know this ho was out of work, so that just goes to show how much I paid attention. I guessed I was too busy being flossy to notice. No one knew I had the money from Selah. Aside from the new car, it was really hard to tell. I was already buying or boosting name-brand shit, so having shit wasn't new to me. I just had more of it now.

"Job where?" I asked, faking interest. I really couldn't care less about anyone else's coin. I had to keep my shit intact.

She wasn't one of my main bitches, so I really didn't keep up with her like that. I really only started hanging out with Tasha and Renee because the hoes

I thought were my main bitches were acting goofy all of a sudden. She lived on my block, and we had been on cool terms since high school. She was a good time if nothing else, and when I wasn't out slumming it in the burbs with Selah and Skye, I was on the block acting ghetto with her. She didn't fit the mold of Selah and Skye, so she was the friend I had on the side. We went to the same parties, fucked some of the same dudes, and hustled the same way. If I were smart, I would have kept her closer.

"Philly Curvy. Ya girl Skye's store! It's about to open soon, and she's looking for people. I slaaaaaayyyyed, bitch! Ya hear me?"

She went on and on about her interview, but I had other shit on my mind. When was Skye going to tell me she was moving forward with the store? I remembered her mentioning it some time ago, but she never said it was coming to fruition. I was irritated all over again.

Gone were the days when me and my girls were tight as Spanx on a fat bitch. This shit was breaking my heart. I was the most fashionable of the three of us. Surely, she needed my expertise and input, right? This bitch didn't even call to ask if I wanted to help. *Sigh*. This shit was killing me slowly. I needed my friends more than they knew.

Taking my contents from the bag, I began the activation process for this little Cricket phone I just purchased from Walmart. I was too scared to keep

Chase's phone on, and I definitely wasn't calling dude from my personal phone. This would be the way we kept in contact. I didn't know if he wanted Chase's phone back, so I planned to use it as collateral. There wasn't really a bunch of deep shit in it, just a bunch of naked pictures of Selah and other random chicks, a few text messages to some bitches I was sure Selah had no clue about but were irrelevant now because his dumb ass was dead, and a secret folder that I didn't know the password to.

I wondered what was in there and definitely tried to crack the code on more than one occasion. I was planning to mention it to Goon to see if he would take the bait. Chase had an entire operation going on. Surely there was something worthwhile in this damn phone.

"Hey, let me hit you right back. I gotta take a shit," I butted in. I didn't hear 90 percent of what the hell she said anyway.

So I'd been thinking, did I want my ex-friend dead or not? Yeah, that was some odd shit to be going through someone's head, but it was the truth. I still couldn't believe she cut me a check for $2 million. *How much did she give Skye? Clearly enough to open a damn store.* I wanted to ask her without being messy, but then again, I didn't know what my reaction would be if she said some astronomical amount that I wasn't ready to hear.

Hell, maybe we all just needed to hug it out and start over. Grabbing my phone from my purse, I scrolled through until I got to Skye's number. I was hesitant but pressed the talk option anyway. The worst she could do was not answer.

"Hey, sis!" Skye answered the phone in a better mood than expected. That shit caught me off guard. I didn't know why I thought she would be sounding like Selah. It wasn't her boyfriend and sister who were murdered. I decided to roll with it and see where this took me. *I just might be getting one of my friends back.* Once I got her on board, she could talk to Selah, and we'd be good to go.

"Hey! I hear congrats are in order," I replied, hoping to keep the conversation upbeat.

"Congrats?" She sounded puzzled, like she didn't know what was going on in her life.

"Your store! I hear it's going to be opening soon."

"Oh, yeah, thanks. I'm trying to get it together." The shade. She wasn't even going to say anything to me about the shit. *I can't believe this is where we are in our friendship right now.* "How did you find out? I wasn't going to say anything until it was time for my grand opening. Didn't want to jinx it."

Okay, pump your brakes, Vice. She wasn't trying to play you. Or was she?

"One of my homegirls came in for an interview earlier. She was hype telling me about it. Renee Wallace."

"Yasssss, Renee came to slay, baby. I gave her a box of clothes and a naked mannequin, and she went to work! I'm thinking about making her my manager."

She was going on about how well she did and the other people she had to interview, but I couldn't care less about it. I wanted to know where we were in all of this.

"I'm just trying to make sure this couple million stretches, honey. This has to work. Once I leave my job, there's no turning back."

"She gave you two million?" I tossed into the atmosphere to let her know I caught that tea. Shit, she gave me two too. Actually more, considering that first drop. I wondered how she would feel knowing that.

"Yeah, ain't that what you got?"

"For sure," I lied. I'd save that little bit of info until later. "She really did an equal split, but that ain't why I called you."

"Facts," she replied with a slight laugh. "Anyhoo, what's going on in your world?"

"Just trying to decide what I want to do. Are you interested in partnering up? I'm thinking about getting into jewelry."

The lies were rolling out tonight. I was on a damn roll. I wondered how hard it would be to convince her to join me into trying to get more money from Selah. Her loyalty to us was to a fault, and it was annoying sometimes. We chatted a little more about these fake plans I had before her man started calling.

"Okay, girl, let me get this store closed so I can get out of here. I'll keep you posted on everything. I love you, okay? Things won't be like this forever. We just have to give it some time."

"I love you too, sis." I needed to hear that. That shit definitely brought me to tears . . . momentarily. I loved Skye, and Selah, but a conversation needed to be had before shit got ugly. Deciding to go ahead and make the call, I programmed the name Goon in as the only contact I had in this phone. I swallowed my fear and made the connection.

"Save this number. We will talk soon," I said when he answered. I hung up before he had a chance to respond. He was probably tired of my ass, but I needed him to understand who was in control here. The minute he thought he had the upper hand, it would change the dynamic of what was happening here, and I wasn't about to let that go down.

Making sure the house was secure, I lay in bed and began searching Zillow for properties I could afford. I had a feeling shit was about to get hot in the hood, and I needed to bounce before the flames came this way.

Chapter 11

Skye

Stay in Your Lane, Sis

I'm about to be a mom.

As much as I wanted to care about this dry-ass beef that was going on between Selah and Vice, I really couldn't find it in me to give a damn about any of it. It was just all too much for no real valid reason at all. In all honesty, we wouldn't be going through this shit had Selah done right by us and just split the money equally. Well, we wouldn't be going through this shit at all had we not killed people, but you get what I'm saying. Our beef wasn't about the deaths of our loved ones. It was over greed. Yeah, she hooked us up, but she played in Vice's face, and I could totally understand her reason for being upset.

Vice was the real crazy one in the group. Like "certified with papers" crazy. I wouldn't be surprised if she was in the midst of setting Selah's ass up as we spoke. I didn't put nothing past Vice, which was why I always kept her close. Love her like a sister? For sure. Kill her like an enemy? Without blinking a fucking eye. With people like us, it has to be understood that you do one of two things: get that bitch or get got by that bitch. It's a snap decision, no hesitation allowed. It could definitely cost you your life.

I had bigger fish to fry though. I was in the final stages of opening my store, and all of a sudden, I was getting cold feet. This wasn't a hefty investment. I still had plenty of money left if this didn't work out. My issue was that I would be dropping this load in about three months. That wasn't really enough time in my head to get things in a rhythm that I liked. I basically had to build trust with people I didn't know to run my store while I was on maternity leave. Bitches steal. I knew this firsthand. I was the best who had ever done it and not gotten caught. So how could I make sure my dream didn't crash and burn while I was gone?

Selah was supposed to be helping me with this, but she was five steps from being committed to a loony bin. Her unstable ass was not ready for what I needed her to do. Last I talked to her, she still couldn't sleep at night without nightmares, but she did give me her share of the investment, so I guessed I couldn't complain too much. I needed someone who was on point. Her ass wasn't it. I could have asked Vice, but she was out living her best or worst life and definitely didn't have time to be working for me. She'd fuck around and be laundering money through the business or some shit. My boyfriend had his own job that he thought he needed because, as far as he was concerned, I was still working my regular job full-time.

I dropped down to part-time the minute the check cleared, from Selah to keep my benefits. I found out I was pregnant shortly after, and even though I could afford it, I wasn't about to pay out of pocket to have a baby. He would want to know where I got the money from, and I wasn't about to divulge that type of info to anybody walking the planet. You would think I would be happy right now, but in these moments, I was reminded that I was really out here in these streets by myself. I didn't have anyone. Trust me, I cried plenty of nights because of it. Everyone kept saying it was the hormones, and maybe it was. But the reality was that all I had was my baby, and he or she wasn't even here yet. Aside from Selah and Vice, I didn't have anybody to get hype with me about this baby coming. I hadn't seen my cousins since we were little, and their parents let me go into foster care when my mom fucked up and lost custody of me. As far as I was concerned, me and my fake-ass family didn't have a damn thing to talk about. Once they put me away, I stayed away, but it would have been nice if at least one of them came to look for me. It was definitely out of sight, out of mind for me and them, and although I wasn't cool with it, I accepted it for what it was and did my best to never need they ass.

When I first got pregnant, I was scared to death. It happened at a time that just wasn't conducive to bringing a child into the world, but I quickly realized this was exactly what I needed. Finally, I would have someone who would love me unconditionally. Hugging my stomach, something I did a lot nowadays, I got up and started getting myself together to go down to the store. It was really starting to come together. Some of my inventory had started to come in, and I wanted to start interviewing for staff so that we could get the store up and running soon. My grand opening was slated to happen in a few weeks, and I wanted everything to be perfect.

The Fashion District opened at 10:00 a.m. to the public. I had interviews scheduled starting at eleven, and I didn't want to feel rushed. This baby definitely liked breakfast, and if I didn't eat, I'd be sick the entire day. I was only seven months, but my stomach looked like I was further along or carrying twins. I had a hell of a wobble that everyone found cute but me. I struggled but was dressed and out the door in record time. Parking my car on Fifty-second and Sansom Streets, I wobbled around the corner and hopped on the Blue Line heading to downtown Philadelphia. I got off at Eighth Street, grabbed my grub from Dunkin', and got to the store just in time to see the nice security guard who always seemed to be just walking by when I needed the gate pulled up.

"Let me get that for you, ma," he said, bending to unlatch the gate from the floor. Why they had the lock so far down was lost on me. We joked about it often.

"Thank you so much. This baby definitely wasn't letting me be great today." I smiled, stuffing the key in my fanny pack so that I wouldn't misplace it. It was a $65 charge to replace the locks, and they'd gotten me for that twice already.

He did a sweep of the store to make sure there were no unwanted surprises, and then he was on his way. It'd never happened in my store, but a few of the stores had people in the back who were not supposed to be there and were robbed at gunpoint. No one knew yet how they were getting in and figured it was an inside job. The backs of our stores didn't have any doors that led from the outside, so someone had to be letting these people in. The guard was put on alert after it happened for the third time, and once he learned I was pregnant, he always made sure I was good. I would see him every hour until his shift was over, and he would always come to make sure my gate was closed and locked properly.

I had so many boxes in the back it was overwhelming to look at them all, but I wasn't going to let it stress me out today. That was the purpose of doing the interviews. My goal was to have a skeleton crew in by midweek. I had clothes, shoes, clothes racks, mannequins, everything to get it poppin'. I didn't want my store to look empty like some of the stores I saw in here, so I wouldn't be opening until at least 90 percent of my inventory was in stock.

As the computer booted up, I checked mail, emails, and messages. My website was almost ready to go as well, and I was starting to feel a little excitement. I had models come in to try on the clothes so that my site designer could set up a virtual fashion show on my web page. I was actually on the road to being an entrepreneur. It was both scary and exciting at the same time.

By the time I got done, my first potential employee showed up for her interview. My process wasn't the typical "sit down and talk about yourself, answer questions that are rehearsed, and pray that you get it right" type of interview. Working at Philly Curvy needed to be a vibe. I introduced myself to her, and off the bat, she seemed a little shy. I first took stock of what she had on. We would not wear uniforms. The Philly Curvy rep would need to look the part. My fashionista would know how to put together funky pieces and not be afraid to be bold. Technically, we were stylists. We were dressing the people who came into the store, and we had to know how to pick pieces that flattered the curvy woman, if you will. If you can't dress yourself, how the hell are you going to dress someone else?

She was cute, though. Edges on fleek, light beat to the face, which I appreciated. Steve Madden chunky ankle boot, slim-fit jean, T-shirt that read, "You Want to Be Me," and a gray blazer with lime green patches on the elbows. I was there for it all. She definitely "looked" like someone I would want in the store, but the true test was coming. Her homegirl could have done this look for her and not necessarily her alone. I would know in due time though.

"Good morning," she greeted me with a smile. That gave her a second check. You had to be pleasant when working in customer service. Being angry just wasn't a good vibe. "My name is Renee. I have an interview at eleven a.m."

"Good morning," I returned the greeting. "I'm Skye, and this is my boutique. What are your first thoughts walking in?"

See, I needed creatives in my space. As the consumer, what do you want to see when you walk into a store? That determines how much of your coins you will spend. I wanted Philly Curvy to be the first name to pop in the heads of every thick chick who needed to slay.

As I listened to her describe the store, I took note of her facial expressions. You could see the excitement in her eyes as she mentally laid the store out, even going so far as telling me what should go where and how to set up near the register for impulse buys. I liked this girl already.

"Definitely put the lip gloss by the register. You know we will sell a million of those," she concluded with a smile.

Did I just meet my store manager? This was looking so promising, but I didn't want to get too hype too fast. I did have other prospects coming.

"I totally agree. So as you can see, there's a naked mannequin in the window. I have five boxes by that wall." I pointed over to where the mannequin was. "In these boxes you will find a few pieces, shoes, accessories, et cetera. You have ten minutes to put our girl together for display. Use as little or as much as you want. Your time starts now."

She looked at me like I was crazy for a second, then quickly turned around to assess the boxes. She didn't seem frazzled in the least as she looked through each box and set a few things aside. I sat and watched as she pulled that outfit all the way together, even taking a few minutes to climb up and fix the mannequin's hair. As she stood back and admired her work, she removed the bracelet from her arm and put it on the mannequin to finish the look. It was so hard keeping the smile off my face. This chick did not come to play with these hoes! She gave her a look that was fresh and contemporary and could easily catch the eye of anyone passing by. I was impressed.

"You definitely slayed the look," I responded as I walked a circle around the model. She did the damn thing. This was definitely an outfit I would wear myself. I especially loved how she wasn't afraid to mix bright colors, patterns, and animal prints. "What does your availability look like? I need reliable staff who can be trusted."

"I'm available to start ASAP. I've been working in retail for years, so I know exactly how to function in apparel. You won't be disappointed."

"Sounds perfect. I'll reach out to you before the week is out. The plan is to have the store up and running within the next few weeks. Have you ever planned a grand opening?"

"In fact I have. I bake and do events in my spare time."

Lord, you showed out when you sent this one! I almost broke out in a praise dance in the middle of the store, but these swollen feet wouldn't allow it. I definitely had her in mind for management, unless God was really blessing me today with someone even better. I thanked her for her time and told her I would be in touch. As she was leaving, she went back over to the mannequin and undressed her, returning her to her normal state, even dropping her bracelet in the box of jewelry that was there.

"I don't want anyone getting any ideas," she laughed, understanding the questioning look I had on my face. "Let them dress her to the best of their ability. I look forward to hearing from you." And with that she was gone as quickly as she came.

Yeah, I liked her, and I couldn't keep my smile from showing this time. I wrote "manager" next to her name as I prepared to meet the rest of the applicants.

It wasn't a bad day after all. I interviewed ten people total. Three of the ten had no clue, and I knew for sure they wouldn't get a call back. I marked a line through their names immediately. I was all for individual style, but some of these outfits had no rhyme or reason. The one chick just had a nasty attitude, and that just wasn't the vibe I wanted in my store. These chicks needed to get along for the sake of the customers. I wasn't saying to be besties, but we needed harmony within these walls.

Just as I was gathering my stuff up to go, my security guard friend came up in time to lock the door for me. I wondered about him briefly but wouldn't dare ask. I didn't want him to think I was shooting my shot. He was just so nice. Young guy, maybe in his thirties. I didn't see a wedding ring, but that didn't really mean shit. He just had a cool vibe about him. He would be perfect to get Selah out of her slump. He made sure I had the key back and asked me if I needed an escort to the train.

"I think I got it from here, but I do appreciate your offer. See you in the morning."

"Same time, same place," he responded as he strolled off.

I hustled as fast as I could to the train, and hurried home to process my day. I wanted to call Selah and Vice to tell them all about it, but quickly dismissed that thought. I wanted to remain smiling, so I would just talk with them about it when it was time for the opening.

When I got down the way, I noticed a lot of police activity going toward where I lived. There was always something happening in the hood, but I hadn't received any calls, so I wasn't too worried. As I got closer to home, I saw that the top of the block near my house was taped off. My heart started beating faster in my chest as I hurried to park the car around the corner. I couldn't get out of the car fast enough as I wobbled as fast as I could up the block. I saw the body covered in a sheet in front of my house, but I needed to get closer. Who the hell was it?

Before I could take another step, the police began pushing me back, and my neighbors started grabbing on me. No one said it, but my gut was telling me that the love of my life was under that sheet. I felt myself overheating, and I started to feel lightheaded. The last thing I remembered was grabbing my belly before falling to the ground surrounded by pitch-black silence.

Chapter 12

Selah

In Your Time of Need

"Please tell me this isn't real."

There was just too much death and too many unfortunate circumstances happening in my life right now. By the time I got done with Vice, all I could do was come home and lie down. Would I ever lead a normal life again? My therapist made the assumption that I would, but I just couldn't see it happening. Not when every time I went out the door I felt like someone was hunting me. My mom being one step from crazy wasn't making it better. I was so frustrated that she wouldn't go to therapy. Clearly, she needed it. Her daughter was dead. Trying to get her to understand that part had me in here pulling my damn hair out. I mean, she knew Sajdah was not coming back, but she wasn't willing to accept it. This shit was draining me like you wouldn't believe. Yet I just let her do what she wanted, and I tried to be there for her the best I knew how. Lately, I'd been feeling like enough was enough. Maybe I didn't, but my dad deserved some peace.

"Ma, I really would like for you to go to therapy with me. I need your support."

I'd tried guilting her. I'd tried tricking her. I tried having civilized conversations with her over an early dinner as she sifted through the growing collection of home improvement magazines that were gathered around her on the table. It was like she took a day out of her life and subscribed to every magazine on the market. I understood that was her way of coping, but it wasn't healthy. She needed to let her feelings out. My dad wanted her to. We both did. I didn't necessarily want her to forget Sajdah, but I wanted her to get her life back. Life after death is harder than people give it credit for. Things would never be how they were before, but we had to pick up the pieces and continue with what was left of our existence.

"Will therapy bring my baby back?" she paused to ask, making eye contact that made me super uncomfortable. She was dead-ass serious. I was dead-ass not ready for the question. She had the nerve to look irked, like I was badgering her or something.

"Mom, it won't. But it will help to get your feelings out. Maybe move toward some normalcy," I tried. I just wanted her better.

"This might just be the new normal, love bug. Maybe I'll go. Let me think about it, since you and your father are so persistent about it."

I glanced at my dad real quick to see if he caught that shade. The look on his face showed that he definitely did, but we both knew a response wasn't the way to handle it. It would just trigger my mom into a fit that neither of us had the strength to handle at the moment, and from the way this conversation was going, she was most likely on her way to snapping out on both our asses. I continued eating my food in silence as she happily flipped through design spreads. I had my own shit I needed to get through, like them damn tapes.

I actually started watching last night. I got through about fifteen minutes before I had to turn it off. Hearing his voice again sent chills through my body. I was hoping there was no audio and I could just watch it in silence, but there it was loud and clear, and I didn't even have the strength to turn the TV down.

Chase was so handsome. I loved everything about him. His walk, his talk, his smell, the sex. The way my body responded when I saw him was crazy. My clit immediately started to pulse, and my nipples got hard instantly. I felt bad just thinking about it. It felt so vivid, like he was in the room with me. As the video played, I lay back on the bed and pretended my hands were his. I found my clit quickly, dipping my fingers inside of my walls, and dragging the

juices up to swirl. I pretended his mouth was placing
soft kisses on me as I whispered in his ear how much
I loved him and how much I missed him. I apologized
as best I could for killing him before tears began to
sting my eyes.

I was damn near close to orgasm until I saw him
on the television pull up with some random female
in the car. That shit blew my entire vibe. Leaning
up, I looked to see what the date was on the screen.
It was at the very beginning of our relationship, so I
cut him a little slack. He was still on the chase then
and hadn't yet claimed me as his. Staring at the girl,
I tried to place her face. Philly is small. I wondered
if I had seen her somewhere before. I was cool with
watching them get out of the car, but when he took
and bent her over the hood right outside, I was done.
They couldn't wait until they got in the house? I was
sure the neighbors in the adjacent buildings saw
this shit. Thankfully he never treated me like that,
but just seeing him with someone else pissed me off.
Reaching for the remote, I clicked the TV off. I'd have
to get back to this some other time.

Lying here just taking it all in, I wondered if I'd
ever find love again. Had I really found it with Chase?
He definitely gave me what I thought I needed at the
time, but was it really love? Or was I trying to talk
myself out of these feelings to justify what I did to
him? This was all just too much. Deciding a shower
would help me out, I got up and forced myself to do

something. I made my shower quick. I hated being alone in any room longer than I needed to be. I felt like Sajdah was always lurking and watching me, and I promise I never believed in ghosts until now.

When I got out of the shower, I saw that I had several missed calls from Skye. I took my time moisturizing my body, promising to get back to her when I was done. I knew she was excited about interviewing a few people today, and I figured she was probably just calling me to talk about it. Just as I was finishing up, the phone started ringing again. Picking it up, I saw that it was Skye again. My stomach instantly tightened into knots. She was too early on in her pregnancy to have the baby.

"Hey, sis! Sorry, I was in the shower," I answered, trying to keep it light in case I was overreacting.

"He's gone. They took him from me!"

"Who's gone? What happened?" I could hear the sobs in her voice, and they pulsed their way through my entire body. I began throwing on whatever I could find so that I could get out of the house.

"They took him. Why?"

"Where are you now? I'm on my way," I said as I made my way down the steps. She was speaking in circles, and I didn't know what the hell was going on.

"Penn. They brought me to Penn."

"Okay, I'll be there soon."

I had no clue what I was rushing to, and I was so afraid to find out. Was this karma? They say the energy you put out you get back tenfold. Was this backlash for what we did to Chase and Sajdah? Technically, Skye never did a thing if we were going to talk about it. She never pulled the trigger. She was just always there to clean up the mess. I didn't know what was happening to my friend. I just knew I had to get to her as quickly as possible.

I pulled up to Penn Medicine almost a half hour later and was ushered back to her room by a nurse. She looked a mess. Eyes puffy, hair disheveled, but the baby was still in her belly. I breathed a small sigh of relief because that would have been a hard pill for her to swallow.

"I'm here, sis." I ran up to the side of her bed. She fell into my arms in a crying fit that brought tears to my eyes. What happened? How did she end up here?

"They took him, sis. He's gone!"

"Who's gone?"

"Tommy. They took my baby's father!"

I was stuck! When the hell did this happen? It was probably on the damn news, and I missed it while I was washing or watching the video.

"Who? What happened, Skye?"

She began telling me how she was having a great day, and once she got home from work, she walked up to his body covered in front of her door. There was a shootout on her block earlier, and he got caught in the crossfire. Witnesses said he had nothing to do with it. He was just on his way in the house. Literally he had just parked his car and was walking up to the porch when the shots rang out. He caught one right to the head and dropped instantly.

I instantly wanted to go spray the neighborhood. These dudes killed me with they non-aiming asses. They probably hit everything but the intended target. Now my girl was left to raise her son by herself. Fucking punks!

"Was he the intended target?"

"I'm not sure. From the little info I got before the ambulance pulled away, he was innocent. They took him from me, sis. Why does God keep taking people from me?"

I just held her in my arms and let her get it all out as I vowed to never leave her alone for as long as I could. I had my family. I couldn't imagine how life was for her, but I'd do my best to be by her side. That's what friends are for, right?

Chapter 13

Goon

The Eagle Has Landed

There's something about the air in Philly. It's a little grimy, tinged with a little crime and a lot of love. It was a little bit of just what I needed. I didn't realize how much I missed home until I looked out the window and could see Southwest Philly in the distance. I hated flying, but all my worries went away as soon as the plane hit the ground at Philadelphia International Airport. I was home, and I couldn't wait to see my family.

No one knew I was coming, so this was even better. I mentioned it to my granny, but I never gave her a date, so she would definitely be stoked to see me when I arrived. I didn't want her having the entire neighborhood at the house when I arrived. For sure she would have had the grill going and everything. I would have appreciated the love and the excitement, but I needed this trip to be low-key. I was here to handle business. I'd reach out to the family at a later date. Checking to make sure I still had my house key, I gathered my carry-on from the overhead and made my way out of first class to get my suitcase from the carousel.

Yeah, I could have stayed in a hotel, but literally there was no place like home. I tried to get my grandmother to move out of the hood, but she refused to budge. Oftentimes she told me she was rooted here. Everyone she loved and knew was there. Philly was her home.

"I raised nine kids and five grandkids in this house, and we never missed a meal," she would tell me proudly every time I sent her a new house listing. I wanted her in Miami with me, but I knew if no one else, her church family had her. Removing her from what she knew wouldn't have made her happy at all. So she stayed, and I just made sure all of her bills were paid and that she had what she needed in her account. The first thing I did when I got my first check from the NBA was pay her house off. That way she never had to worry about having a roof over her head.

I had an account set up for her that she had the card to, and I just slid her money over there monthly. I never put more than $1,000 or so in it at a time. I remembered the first time I put $100,000 in the account, and she lost her mind. Granny wasn't used to seeing that kind of money all at once. She refused to take all of it, and after a lengthy discussion, I agreed to write a check for half the amount to the church, and I just siphoned the rest to her over time. Surely my contribution to the Lord's house earned me some brownie points for having to put the fool who killed my boy into the ground right next to him, right? I'd have to look into that at a later date. For now, I just wanted to get to my first love as quickly as possible.

As I walked to collect my luggage, I could feel the stares coming from the people around me. No, I didn't travel with security, so anyone could walk right up to me if they wanted to. Now don't get me wrong. Everyone knew who number 17 was on the court. I was a beast with the ball. However, I was very humble, and I knew where my support came from. I felt the eyes, but I never initiated contact or conversation. I would just toss a smile out and keep moving.

Scrolling through my phone as I waited for my luggage to come down, all of a sudden, I felt a weight around my calf. I stood at six feet four inches, so most people were shorter than me, but not that short. When I looked down, I saw the prettiest brown eyes staring back at me. She had to have been about 2 years old, and I fell in love instantly. I couldn't wait for my baby to get here. Scooping down to pick her up, I saw her mom rushing over to grab her with a concerned look on her face.

"I'm so sorry," she apologized as she reached for her little girl. "I sat her down for one second, and before I knew it, she was gone."

"It's no problem. They are quick on those little legs," I said as I smiled and gave her back to her mom. She talked to me in baby talk as she slobbered and squirmed, reaching her little chubby hands out for me to hold her again. It was seriously the cutest thing ever. It also made me sad because my brother would never experience moments like this. Whoever took him out robbed him of everything. Mom thanked me again and went back to gathering her things to go, this time securing the baby in a stroller before getting her other items together. I smiled as I watched them walk away, picturing my girl just like this in a few years.

Finally, my bag surfaced, and I grabbed it quickly and walked toward the car rental hub to pick up my wheels for the weekend. I saw the looks. Some were not sure if it was really me. Others knew for sure but were afraid to approach me. None were as brave as the little girl who just ran up and grabbed me. Either way, I was just trying to get the hell up out of the airport and on my way.

Once I secured the ride, I was on my way to the place where I knew that, if things didn't work out, I could always come back to. I was nostalgic riding around the hood. *Seems like forever since I've been down here.* I was shocked by the way things were looking around here. Philly was starting to remind me of Baltimore. It was looking like a ghost town. Full of crime and neglected. Luckily both cities had people who were determined to keep them afloat. Thank God for prayer, because politics were getting us nowhere.

As I weaved my way around the city, I took note of who and what I saw. As far as I was concerned, anyone in the city could have killed Chase. Anyone in this city could catch this fire, too: blind, crippled, crazy, 8 to 80. Whoever did it had it coming. I took note of how the houses changed the closer I got to the hood. Although they were all row homes, they looked a lot nicer near the airport. Korman Suites had the game on lock over there. The hood changed from nice row homes to blocks with one house on them and the rest condemned as I got to Southwest Philadelphia. Around Fifty-second and Pine the houses got big again, and the neighborhood got a little nicer again as you got closer to Cobbs Creek. Finding a spot on the 6200 block of Washington Avenue, I grabbed my bag and made my way to my childhood home.

I could smell the coffee, sausage, and eggs from her early morning breakfast even before I got fully in the house. My grandmother had been waking up at five in the morning for as long as I could remember. I set my bags down as quietly as possible so that I could sneak up on her. I removed my shoes as well because Granny did not play tracking the outside through her living space. As I approached the kitchen, I could hear Wendy Williams playing on the television she had wall mounted across from the kitchen table. I chuckled as I realized things hadn't changed. Grandma loved her trash TV.

"Whoever you are, make yourself known before you catch these hands," came Grandma's voice from the kitchen. The biggest smile broke out on my face as I rounded the corner and came into view. "Oh! Baby boy, why didn't you tell me you were coming?"

She jumped up from the table and rounded it quickly, giving me the most heartfelt hug. I didn't even know I needed it until then. I held on to her for dear life. I needed to make up for all the hugs I missed over the months. I stepped back and just looked at her. She didn't look a day over 45, and she had just turned 75 this year. Skin soft and silky feeling, chunky from age, hair nice and healthy. Grandma was still living her best life even though her kids, and I was sure we (her grandkids) ran her ragged.

"I'm just in town for a few days, Gram. Looking into some properties and other things," I partially lied to her.

"I'm not moving, so don't start your mess," she said firmly but lovingly. "Sit. Let me make you a plate."

Before I could decline, she got busy moving around the kitchen, quickly filling my plate with a nice home-cooked meal. Baby, she could burn! I devoured my plate, afterward helping her get the kitchen back in order. My phone was burning a hole in my pocket. I needed to let the crew know I touched down, but my grandma deserved my undivided attention. She was my everything, and respectfully, I wanted her to have her time with me and me with her.

Once we were done in the kitchen, I went and gathered my belongings while she called her home-girls, excited to let them know I was in town. I could see that she had done a few upgrades on the house. It looked like home, but an updated version. My room was untouched, but dust free. Everything was just the way I left it, down to the full-sized bed and the posters on the walls. Just as I was getting ready to head down memory lane, my phone began to vibrate against my leg. I grabbed it quickly, forgetting that I never called to let my girl know I landed safely. When I looked at the screen, it was the number of the bitch who called me the other day. I was not in the mood for her shit today, but I had to keep her in my corner until I figured out how she fit in this puzzle.

"Yeah," I spoke into the phone. I was not in the mood for pleasantries with this broad. Depending on how this went, she would more than likely end up in the ground just on GP. She thought she had me, but low-key, the minute I got the drop on her ass, it would be over.

"Hey, stranger, just making sure to stay in touch with you. We need to have a conversation soon."

"That we do," I agreed. Keeping it short and sweet with her was the easiest way for me to keep my attitude in check. I couldn't kill who I didn't know, right?

"Okay, cool. I'm busy right at the moment, but I will be in touch."

I just hung up. I scrolled through my contacts and made another call.

"Yo, bro. I'm here."

"Perfect. I'm on my way to you."

We hung up the phone, and I put my things away so that my grandmother didn't have to fuss over me. By the time I got back in the living room, two of her church friends were in the living room all sipping tea. They were like my other grandmothers in the church, and I loved them all deeply, I just couldn't get caught up in conversation with them at the moment.

"And there he is! You are just as handsome as you want to be!"

I hugged each of them and politely excused myself so that I could be outside when my boy pulled up.

I could hear his car from around the corner blasting that Meek Mills. I swore he only listened to Philly artists. I got in and turned the volume down a tad and ignored his side-eye from my doing so.

"The eagle has landed," he said as he pulled off.

"Indeed."

Chapter 14

Vice

From One Heaux to Another

I saw on the news that there was a shooting near Skye's house. Her phone had been going to voicemail all afternoon. At first I wasn't concerned. The reception on the Blue Line was trash until you got back outside. I sent her a few texts letting her know I was trying to get in touch, but by the time night fell and I still hadn't heard from her, I was on pins and needles. I broke down and called Selah, and this ho didn't answer either. I was starting to feel nauseated from the anxiety and decided if no one called me I would start calling the hospitals. Skye didn't fuck with her family at all, so it wasn't like I could call them. I just needed to know that she was okay, and then we could get back to this original beef already in progress.

I waited another two hours before I began to call around. I started downtown at Jefferson and worked my way up to the University of Penn. She had to be somewhere between Center City and West Philly. I had to pretend like I was a family member, and I lucked out finding her at Penn Hospital in the emergency room. I jumped up and immediately made my way across the city. I didn't know if something happened to her or the baby, and since she wasn't answering, I needed to go make sure everything was kosher.

When I got to the hospital, I gave my information at the desk, and I was escorted back to the area she was being held in. They were so ghetto at this hospital. She would have been better off in the county at Lankenau. As I stopped to get some hand sanitizer, I could hear what sounded like Skye and Selah talking. I stepped just a little closer so that I could hear better, just to be sure I wasn't trippin'.

"So you're not going to talk to her anymore? You know it was more than about the money," I heard Skye say to whoever she was talking to. I was waiting to hear the other voice before I just assumed it was squad.

"Man, fuck that bitch. I promise it look like her ass on them tapes from Chase's house, but it's at nighttime, and I can't get a good view of her. The shape definitely looks like her, but I can't get a good view of her face. I still got some more video to watch, so

I won't claim it yet. Just know if it is her, she will be the last body I catch before I move," Selah responded.

"I can't take no more death, Selah. These fools done took my baby's father away from me. We need each other right now," Skye pleaded with her.

"Naw, sis. We got each other. That one right there I'll keep close until I can't."

I didn't even bother to stay for the rest of the conversation. These bitches were plotting on me, and trust, before they got the drop on me, I'd be on their ass like hot grits. I was shocked that I even started crying about this shit. I was stronger than this, but I felt so betrayed. How was me wanting a fair cut causing so much animosity? Furthermore, I never even thought about her actually looking at the tapes one day.

Fuck! I may have to get these hoes right quick. It was looking more like I was going to have to leave the city sooner than I thought. Making a beeline for the exit, I grabbed my whip from valet and headed back to the crib. Now that I knew how they were moving, I had to play them closer than they thought they were playing me. This shit hurt me to the core, but it was all good. There's no honor among thieves. Always remember that.

When I got back home, I ran into the house, all of a sudden very paranoid about being in the streets. I was getting angrier by the second. Like, did these hoes turn on me? We were in this shit until the end.

It wasn't about to be the end for me. Damn that shit. Just as I was losing it, my phone began to chirp in my purse. Running over to my bag, I pulled it out only to see Skye calling me. I rolled my eyes so damn hard but answered anyway.

"Hey, love! I've been calling you for hours! Are you okay?" I asked, feigning interest in her well-being. It was probably more Selah than her, but she never checked that bitch properly, and I was over it at this point. The "quiet friend" shit was played out.

"Yes and no," she said with a tear-filled voice. "My baby father was killed in front of my house. I saw him when I got home. I must have fainted, because when I woke up, I was here in the emergency room."

"I heard there was a shooting over that way. I didn't know it was him. I'm so sorry that happened, friend." I hoped I sounded sincere. Honestly, I couldn't care less. Mofos die daily. We were responsible for a few. "How is the baby?" I asked. Now I would feel terrible if she lost her man and her child. That's just wrong on so many levels, but karma shows up like that sometimes, and we are never ready to deal with it.

"He's fine. She's fine. I don't know what I'm having," she explained through a small giggle. "They've been monitoring me since I got here. I didn't land on my stomach, and I believe someone caught me on the way down. I should be going home by the morning."

"Okay, that's good news. I'm glad to hear you're okay."

"I am. I will be. We all need to hook up and put these shenanigans to the side," she said.

"I agree. Let's just get through one tragedy at a time."

We spoke for a little while longer and then said our goodbyes. Not long after we hung up my phone rang again, and it was Skye again.

"Hello?"

"I don't even know why you called that ho. All of that shit was so fake. If she really gave a fuck about you, she would have her ass up here," I could hear Selah saying.

"Big. Fucking. Facts. And to think I was riding with her to get more from you. She better do right with what she got. I know I am. I just need to make sure me and my seed are on a bean."

"Oh, you will never have to worry about that. My godson will be well taken care of. There's another check where that last one came from, sis. You're more responsible than Vice's slow ass, but it's all good. Like I said, the minute I can prove what I saw, it's on and poppin'."

These bitches . . . It just went to show that you can only trust a bitch as far as you can throw her. I wouldn't be surprised if she got her own dude set up. Who the fuck just loses their other half and sits in the hospital plotting against someone you call your friend? Something about it wasn't right, but I had something for her ass.

"Hey, Renee," I spoke into the phone after pulling up my homegirl's number. "Did you ever hear back about that job at the boutique?"

"No, not yet. Hopefully I will hear something soon. I really need the gig."

"Listen, I got a few dollars for you to make once you get the gig. Keep me posted."

Hanging up the phone, I began to plot my get-back. If they thought they were going to one-up me, they had another think coming. I'd never been the one to play with, and I saw I had to remind these bitches of exactly who I was. This shit hurt, but I'd be fine. My mom always taught me that being my own best friend trumped all else. That was a lesson I'd never forget.

Chapter 15

Selah

Say It Ain't So

Who in the hell would want to shoot Dave? I mean, he was definitely in these streets, but not like the trappers we knew. He was more of the friendly neighborhood drug dealer you turned up at the parties with. At the most, he was probably selling loud. He wasn't moving no real weight or no hard-core shit last I knew about it. It was hard seeing my friend like this. *I must look just like her with Chase and my sister gone.* This entire situation was a mess, and I was beyond irritated that Vice didn't even show her face once she found out Skye was in the hospital. She could have lost her baby in the process. All this bitch did was send a few texts and this dry-ass phone call after Skye insisted on calling her. She was so irking, but it was okay. She had hers coming.

I had to get back to those tapes. That was the only thing consuming me nowadays. I saw the trail of girls who came and went through Chase's house. Some were from before we got together. All came before I actually made the move in with him, with the exception of Sajdah, but we were definitely in deeper. A few times I even saw my sister in the video during the day when she was supposed to be at work. I only knew it was her and not me because the time stamps were times when I was definitely on the job, and if need be, I would use that fact in court. She said he chose her. Maybe there was some truth to it. She was surely there enough to prove it. She had a key code and everything. I hadn't gotten that far into the tapes, but I'd already counted her showing up at his house on at least a dozen or more different occasions. I was the fucking side jawn to my sister's relationship with Chase, and that shit hit me like a ton of bricks. Shit, could he even tell the damn difference in the beginning? How did he know who he had and when?

Yet it didn't make a lick of sense. He gave me the keys to the crib, and the ring. What was the damn purpose of me if he had the identical me at his beck and call? I had video of inside the house that I was scared to damn watch for fear that I would see the two of them together. There wasn't shit more I could do to either of their asses now. I already did the damn most, but solidifying what I didn't want to acknowledge was killing me softly.

Sigh.

I needed to be there for my friend like she was there for me, and that was what I would be focusing on at the moment. After making sure she was settled in for the night, I got my car out of valet parking and made my way home. So many things were going through my mind. The fragile mental state of me, my family, and my friends. The possibility of starting over in another city so that I didn't have the constant reminders. The guilt of leaving my mom and dad behind, even though my dad was okay with me moving on with my life. I even thought about asking Skye to come along with me, but I knew she wouldn't just leave her dude and her store behind. Maybe after his funeral I could get her to change her mind. We didn't have to go far, just out of this area. Once she got a trustworthy manager, the store could run itself.

Sigh, again. It was just all too much.

Pulling over at the gas station, I decided to top my tank off since I was out here. I wasn't driving too many places these days, but I liked to have my tank full just in case I needed to drive to Africa or some shit. When I got out, I noticed a lot of guys in the store, and some onlookers outside the store. It made me nervous, and I started to just leave, but I didn't feel like waiting to get what I needed. I needed some snacks, too, so I just sucked it up, grabbed only the card that I would be using and my phone and keys, and went inside.

All of the guys in the store stopped and looked at me when I walked in. I was used to it, so I just kept it moving. Even in my most depressed state, I was still cute as fuck. I grabbed some ice cream, a few bags of chips, and a beverage and made my way up the store honestly oblivious to all the stares. I got in line to pay for my stuff, and as I was leaving one guy in particular caught my eye. I couldn't connect how I knew him, but he definitely looked vaguely familiar. The way everyone was gawking at him, I figured he was someone important. He was definitely tall as shit, so he was probably some hood celebrity on the courts.

Anyhoo, making a hasty exit, I pumped my gas, declining several offers for one of the homeless people hanging around the pumps to do it for me. I could feel the anxiety creeping up the back of my neck, and this was not the place to start spazzing out. My chest got so tight, and I could barely breathe. I didn't even get all of the gas I paid for as I clumsily put the pump back and climbed back inside of my vehicle. I called my dad, but when he answered, I couldn't say anything.

"Baby girl, just take a deep breath. Are you in a safe place?"

"Yes," I managed to squeak out. The tears were starting to blur my vision, and I just wanted to get home.

"Okay, I'll stay on the phone with you. Wipe your face, catch your breath, and drive carefully. If you feel too overwhelmed, just pull over in a well-lit area, and I'll come get you."

I put my dad on speakerphone and began to move the vehicle. I caught eye contact with the really tall guy from the store once more as people circled around him to get autographs. He looked at me like he knew me too, and that shit made me so nervous. I wanted to put my finger on who he was, but not right now. I was focused on getting the hell home unscathed. I kept looking in the rearview, making sure no one was following me as I tried not to go over the speed limit. These county cops be bored, and I just couldn't do it tonight.

When I pulled up to the house, my mom and dad were outside waiting for me. I felt so relieved to see them both. I jumped out of my car and ran into their arms. Lord, the world was such a scary place when you had demons on your neck constantly. They both assured me everything was fine and that I was safe.

When I got inside, I hopped in the shower to get myself together, and I laid my head on my mom's lap once I got my pajamas on. She didn't ask me for an explanation, and I didn't offer one. I just knew that I needed to get control of my life at some point. As my mom sang to me a song that she used to sing to me and Sajdah as kids when we were too restless to sleep at night, I didn't even try to stop my tears as I let her comfort me, and I felt normal for a second and not like the person who killed her daughter.

By the time I made it up to my room I felt a little better. I lay in bed and didn't even turn the television on this time to keep me company in the dark. As I lay there and scrolled through my phone, I came across a post that caught my eye. It was the guy at the gas station, and someone from my timeline had taken a pic with him and posted it. The hashtag #17 was at the bottom of the post, and when I clicked it, I almost dropped my phone. Came to find out he was the man! Miami Heat number 17 to be exact. But more importantly, I thought he was the friend Chase wanted me to meet some time ago. I wasn't exactly sure, but I would definitely find out. I made myself a note to get up extra early so that I could look more into this. For now I just needed some sleep, and I wanted to get my nightmares over with early tonight.

Chapter 16

Skye

News Flash

Let me just tell you, you find out exactly who's rocking with you in your time of need, honey. My man was shot and killed right in front of my house. From what I heard when I was finally released the next day, his body sat out there for hours before the coroner came to collect it. I could see the bloodstains still on the ground when I got home. There were thirteen circles on the ground from the shell casings the cops collected from the scene. Five more circles were on the porch. I counted three holes on my door. They literally had to have run right up and killed him for the shell casings to be that close to home. I probably would have passed out again if Selah weren't there to catch me. What was the world coming to? I guessed it was a good thing I wasn't home. Whoever did this probably would have gotten both our asses.

None of this shit felt real. When they say that one day you're here and possibly the same day you're gone, it's the real deal. Had I known the last time I saw him would be the last time I'd see him, I would have hugged him a little longer, told him I loved him a dozen more times, lain in bed with him a little while longer. He was snatched from me in a blink of an eye, and I had no clue why. Did he really get caught in a crossfire? Were they chasing someone else? Or was it some neighborhood beef that he never mentioned that took him out? We never discussed what he did in depth. He knew I didn't like it, but he had to do what he knew how to do just like every other guy from the hood. So we just didn't talk about it, and I just prayed without ceasing that he stayed safe. I guessed those prayers landed differently when you were out here killing people your damn self. The blackassity of me to think that I could take life and request protection for the ones I loved to be spared. God had to be looking at me and laughing, but from what I remembered from my church days, he was a forgiving God, so I continued to pray in hopes that one got to Him eventually.

I didn't have anybody. That shit hit like a punch to the throat. I mean, let's face it. Vice was being a dick, and Selah was two steps from being locked down with a 302 on her record. My family had been dead to me for years. You would think at a time like now we would be closer than ever, but everyone just seemed to be absorbed in their own shit. It was fucked up, but it was the reality of the situation. Selah showed up, but only halfway, and I fully understood her plight. I couldn't expect someone to be there for me who needed someone to be there for them at the same time. At the time, aside from feeling her pain for losing Sajdah, I didn't understand what she was going through. Now I got that shit wholeheartedly, and it hurt like hell. The truth? I was left in this big, cold world by my lonesome, and this shit made me sad as fuck. Depression is real, and only for the sake of my baby did I try to squelch those feelings. In reality, he or she was all I had left. I didn't want my child coming into the world anxious, so I decided that once my man was buried, I would need to pull it together. All of that shit sounded amazing in my head, but I knew the execution was going to take some work.

Once I was inside the house, his absence sucked the air out of the room. He was all over the place: boots by the door, jacket on the railing, remnants of weed smoking in an ashtray on the table. I would give anything to fuss at him once more about smoking in the house. The pain felt like ants crawling all over my body, and I felt so weak.

"This shit can't be real," I said more to myself than to Selah. I damn near forgot she was even still here.

"I know your pain, sis. I can stay here with you. Just say the word. Those nights can get real."

Shit, tell me about it. Sajdah and Chase showed they asses up here more than I wanted to admit, and now my son's father was added to the list. I didn't actually pull the trigger on either one of them, but being there made me just as guilty. Guilty by association in fact. Not stopping it made me even guiltier than Selah pulling the trigger. Chase caught me off guard, so I really couldn't be held responsible for that one, but I thought we all had an understanding with Sajdah's situation. So many times when I dreamed about her, she asked me why I didn't help her. I took the money. I deserved the torture.

"You have your own shit going on, Selah. I'll be fine."

"No, you won't. Trust me. I already got a bag packed. I can use the company also. The energy in my house is driving me crazy."

I didn't want her here. I really just wanted to be by myself so that I could take it all in, process what the fuck happened, and try to piece all this shit together, but it seemed like she needed this more than I did, so I let her stay. That was what I did: never saying shit, always bending to accommodate those around me. That shit was going to get me killed one day, and mentally it was draining me. Nevertheless, I didn't say a word. I just let her get comfortable as I made my way up to my room.

Curling up into a ball in the middle of my bed, I just held myself and cried. I wanted to know who did this so I could get their ass, but what could I do pregnant? It felt like the best thing to do was to get back focused with my store so that I could create a promising future for myself and my baby. It'd been kicking a lot lately, and it often reminded me that I had something to look forward to.

I felt like I was in bed forever, and I must have eventually fallen asleep. When I woke up, Selah was in bed next to me, snoring lightly. I stared at her sleeping form in the dark, wondering how she was coping with her demons. I mean, this shit had to be difficult for her. I made a mental note to call Vice in the morning. We needed each other, and all this stupid-ass beef was going to come to an end. Period.

I tried to get comfortable, but going back to sleep didn't seem like an option. My mind was spinning, and deciding to do something constructive with my time, I went ahead and typed my job offer letter up for the few potentials I had. The one girl, Renee, showed up and showed out. I was very impressed with her sense of style and her initiative. I offered her the management position. Hopefully we would be able to build trust so that once I went on leave, I wouldn't have to be stressing about the store. Ideally, I was supposed to be interviewing more people, but instead I had to look into funeral plans for my boyfriend.

When his sister called me while at the hospital, she was very nice, and we offered each other condolences and just chatted about how loved her brother was. His mom was the complete opposite, but he had already warned me about her, and you would think she would have been nicer to me after all this time. We were over a year in at this point. I deserved some props for that, right? I was sure she already made the assumption that I was responsible for his death somehow. She barked at me as soon as I answered the phone, and the only reason why I didn't bang on her ass was because her stance was probably coming from a place of pain.

"I told him not to be over there! Who did this to him?" she demanded like the hell I knew. Shit, if I knew that, I would already be on they ass.

I just let her rant without disruption. Shit, this dude was from K&A (Kensington and Allegheny), also known as Zombie Land. All the dopeheads were from there, and the crime rate was ridiculous. He was just as likely to get killed in his own neighborhood, so being in mine wasn't that much worse. She was hurting, and she was speaking out of anger. She lost her only son. I couldn't even imagine the pain she was in. I let her go on and on, and I offered to pay for his funeral. Hell, I had the money. That was the least I could do.

Now lying on my side, I just scrolled through my phone and looked through old photos of us. I loved that man. He was a thug, but he was so gentle with me. When I met him, I was so broken from previous relationships and lack of family support. All I really had was Selah, Sajdah, and Vice, and they could only do so much. This man made me smile, you hear me? He helped me see my value and gave me something to look forward to every day. He just wouldn't leave those streets alone, but I understood it and didn't try to change him. Too bad I couldn't get him out of the hood before they got to him.

It felt like it took days to come, but sleep finally took over, and the first person I saw was my love. He walked up to me and held me and whispered in my ear that he was at peace. I held on to him so tight as the tears flowed freely. He held me even tighter, and when I finally stepped back to look at him, I could see the blood from where the bullets had penetrated his body. I wanted to cover all the holes with my hands, but there were too many. He assured me that everything was okay as he stepped back and began to walk into the light. Just as I thought I could run and catch up to him, I could see his wings expand. He was in good hands, and good company, and that brought me a little bit of peace before the light shining through the window knocked me back into reality. He was gone.

Chapter 17

Goon

Home Sweet Heartache

"So what's the move for tonight?"

Since I was home, I thought I might as well hit the club scene. It'd been a minute since I let loose a little, and I wanted to see what was really going on in these streets. Philly changed a lot since I'd been gone. The neighborhood that I used to run around as a kid with a snotty nose used to seem so big. Now I felt like I was suffocating on the same block that embraced me with open arms. I couldn't breathe in this house, and the thought crossed my mind a million times since I landed to go grab a hotel room. Just walking up on the steps had me in a chokehold that I couldn't explain. Suffocating . . . in the same house I grew up in. I almost did just that and grabbed a suite in Center City, but I knew it would break my grandmother's heart if I left. She would definitely be offended, and I couldn't do that to her. So I just thugged it out like I did with all situations that had me uncomfortable. I only had to sit in this hell for a few more days. I reminded myself of this every chance I got.

After the night we had, I needed something else to take my mind off the shit that was going on here. When I went to the spot, of course they had some fool from the crew tied up and on the brink of death. There's always someone who wants to test the powers-that-be. Sean, the team captain, said they had to put a few down over the last few months. Dudes had been wilding since Chase's disappearance, and we had to restore order if we wanted to maintain control in these streets. I thought they had this together from the last time I was here, but apparently these guys still wanted to test the waters. They didn't want me to be a part of it, and I appreciated them looking out for my career, but Chase would want order. I had to make sure he got what he wanted since no one here could seem to get it together.

When we got down to the bottom, I first went and checked on Chase's aunt before heading downstairs. She too was worried that Chase hadn't come to see her in a while, and it was hard for any of us to tell her that she'd have to wait until she was dead and gone to see him again. She was told that he went back home for a little while, and they didn't know when he would be back. She stopped talking to her sister, Chase's mom, years ago. She probably would already have the truth if she would just answer the phone. Whenever she saw a New York number come up on the phone, she would ignore the call.

I had only met Chase's aunt twice, so she probably had no clue who I or any of the other guys who came to count money and drugs in this house were. She was smart, though, and knew how to mind her damn business. She never tried to go in the basement as far as anyone knew, and she stayed in her lane. After making sure she was straight, I headed down to the basement to see what the story was this time. I could smell the blood and mold as soon as I opened the door. It made me wonder how many bodies this basement claimed. Their spirits were just trapped in these concrete walls, begging for escape.

When I got downstairs, I could hardly stand the stench or the sight. His face was unrecognizable due to swelling, left eye completely closed, right eye not too far behind it. His bottom lip was triple the normal size, even for a black man, and several teeth were scattered in front of him on the floor. One guy held a pair of bloody pliers, the other a bat. Clearly, they were tag teaming this dude. I didn't know exactly what he did, but I didn't feel bad for him. More than likely he done fucked up the church's money and deserved whatever happened to him.

One thing I could say about us was that we were always fair. We built the business that way from the beginning. No one died who wasn't supposed to. We always gave you enough rope before we kicked the chair. I honestly didn't even want to hear his story, but I listened anyway. To run a successful business, you have to know it all. You don't necessarily have to know how to do it all, but your knowledge base is extra important to being successful. Read that one twice.

"What's your story, man?" I asked him as I made myself comfortable against the wall. I refused to sit anywhere else because, from the smell, I could only imagine the amount of bodily fluid that had been splashed around this space. I didn't want to accidently sit on old brain matter or some shit, figuratively or literally. I wondered briefly if Chase had died down here, but I quickly dismissed the thought.

He had the same story as everyone else I'd ever heard about. They always did whatever it was they did because of some family member, baby mom, or stupidity. At some point you had to learn from the people before you and know that we didn't give a damn about any of that shit. When your time was up, that was the end of it.

As he droned on and on in an effort to save his life, I got a text from homegirl who had Chase's phone. I didn't know her name or anything like that. For now, she had one up on me, but that wouldn't be for long. When I got her ass, she would regret it.

Meet me at Onyx. I'll be there by 11. Just maybe we could meet face-to-face.

Was I ready for that? My entire body went numb at the thought. I didn't know how I would react actually putting a face to the voice. After all, I didn't know what part she played in the entire ordeal. Suddenly I couldn't wait to leave. The time on my phone said 10:15 p.m. That meant I had at least forty-five minutes to make a life-changing decision. Was this chick pulling my chain? What if she didn't show up? It wasn't like I knew who the hell I was looking for, and I wondered if she already knew who I was. All of this was overwhelming, and I suddenly started feeling sick.

"You okay, man?" Demon asked as I looked up to see everyone staring at me. Instantly embarrassed, I tried my best to pull it together right quick. You cannot bleed in front of a shark and expect not to get bitten.

"Never been better," I responded as I straightened back up. "So what are we going to do here? I'm ready to go see what these hoes do down at Onyx."

"That. Fucking. Part," Demon responded as he pulled his weapon from his waist. This nigga was a done bun, and they'd probably find his body floating in the Schuylkill River a week from now bloated and unidentifiable. It looked like they were in the process of pulling his damn teeth out, so they wouldn't even have dental records to compare. *Sigh*. When would they learn?

I started making my way up the steps, and before I got all the way to the top, I saw the flash of a silencer bounce off against the wall shortly before hearing a heavy thud hit the floor. This couldn't be life, and for the first time in years, I was glad I had given this life up years ago. Killing ma'fuckas just wasn't my thing. Yeah, I'd done it more times than I liked to admit, but it never made me feel better. Some of these dudes had people just like my grandmother praying for their soul, and hopefully that was enough to get them to the pearly gates.

Demon caught up with me at the top of the steps, and we quickly decided a shower was in order to get the basement stink off of us before we hit the club for the night. He dropped me off at the crib, and I told him I would meet him there. I didn't want to have to wait for him and whoever else was coming to get ready. I knew the bouncer at Onyx and decided to give him a call to let him know I was in town and the crew and I would be making an appearance. I was down to earth, but we sat in VIP. Just in case some shit popped off, I never mingled with the common folk. You are the company you keep, and I surrounded myself with money be it through drugging or thugging. We conducted ourselves differently, and I just didn't have time for the groupie shit.

When I got back to the house, my granny had already turned in for the night, but I didn't miss that plate that she left for me in the microwave. I slammed the shit quickly before hopping in the shower and getting fresh for the night. Gucci down to the socks, I made sure I smelled amazing and looked even better. Just as I was getting ready to leave, my phone rang, and the biggest smile spread across my face. This woman always showed up at the right time. She was the reason why I moved the way I did. I couldn't let anything crazy happen while I was home. I needed to get back to her in one piece.

"Hey, love," I spoke into the phone, my heart just feeling so full.

"Hey, baby," came the sweetest voice from the other end. I couldn't wait to hold her in my arms again. "How is your trip going?"

"It's going," I responded, purposely leaving out any details. "It feels good to see my granny again and just to be back down the way."

We talked a little more as I went and checked on my granny. Then I made my way out of the house. I didn't want to disturb her sleep, and I didn't want her to be worried that I was leaving so late.

"I love you, baby. I'll be home soon."

"Okay, just be careful. I know you want to know what happened to your friend, but you're still alive, and we need you."

That shit almost brought tears to my eyes. I didn't tell her why I was here, but I obviously didn't have to. She knew her man. What's known doesn't always need to be discussed.

Disconnecting our call, I made my way across the city, taking in the sites as I drove. As much as I loved Philly, I knew I had to hurry up and get the hell up out of here. That feeling of anxiety and suffocation was coming back, and I knew it was a sign that I shouldn't be here.

When I got to the club, I used the valet service. Looking at all the ladies lined up to get in, I wondered which one was her. Was she still in line? Was she already inside? I didn't know her name, because if I did, I would have added her to the VIP list. She was a smart one. She wouldn't give me any info until she was good and ready, but I was tired of this cat-and-mouse game with her.

I made my way to VIP and took a seat as I dapped up a few people I knew. The DJ immediately announced my presence to the club, and the crowd went wild. After all, we did just win the championships. I was sort of a big thing in these streets. It felt good to be appreciated, but as the drinks began to flow, I passed on it all and kept my eye on the crowd. I wasn't about to be caught slipping, and I didn't drink and drive.

It was almost midnight, and I didn't even know what I was waiting for. Just as I was ready to give up, my phone buzzed on my hip, and I saw a text from the number shawty had been calling from.

So you the real deal, huh?

I looked up, and my eyes swept across the room, but there were several chicks on their phones. That text could have come from anyone. Frustrated, I decided not to even reply. She would just piss me off, and this was not the environment to lose my cool in. She was playing with me because she thought she had me, but it was cool. The get-back would be well worth it.

Chapter 18

Vice

Keys to the Kingdom

Onyx was lit! I was out with Renee and a few of her girls from the Vill, trying to replace my friends with hers. This shit sucked. I normally wouldn't even be caught doing no sucka-ass shit like this, but what was I supposed to do? What I had with my girls had been built brick by brick since childhood. Selah and Skye were acting all fragile and shit like we'd never been here before, and it was a little off-putting, to be honest. Okay, so it was her sister. That was different, I guessed. But old boy wasn't even that deep. At least not to me. He wasn't even loyal. Like, the fuck! *All this for a nigga who fucked your sister. Come on, yo. We gotta do better as women.* He didn't deserve her, never did. And her sister was just as much of a snake as him. It was time to move on.

Oh, you think I'm a snake too? Shit, I saved her fucking life if you ask me. Get. You. A. Friend. Like. Me. I don't know how many times and how many ways I got to tell you bitches. If your friend won't put her pussy on the line for you, don't fuck with her. She ain't loyal.

As much as I wished I were out with my girls, settling for these few wasn't that bad. They actually knew how to turn the fuck up. There wasn't no whole bunch of catty shit and bickering. No one asked me what happened to my old crew. We came together and we left together. They were on some baldhead-ho shit just like I was, so it was a judgment-free zone that I felt comfortable with. None of them knew I was sitting on millions, and they didn't need to know, so there wasn't no using me about to happen, although I planned to use their asses to the fullest. None of them knew about the shit with Chase and Sajdah aside from what was in the news when Sajdah's body was found, and they didn't need to know that either. Renee asked me a while ago what happened to Sajdah, but we just kept it moving after some dry-ass answer I gave her. I respected her more for not badgering me about it. We weren't about to drop names and serve tea on my girls, even though they weren't fucking with me like they used to. It was cool. Whatever you were supposed to have always came back to you. You just have to give it time.

Now back to the matter at hand. I didn't know
who I was looking for. Let's keep that in mind. This
dude was just a name in a dead nigga's phone I was
considering extorting. I didn't have a face, just a
damn nickname, because I was sure his momma
didn't name him Goon. Or did she, with her ghetto
ass? Nowadays you really can't be sure. I didn't know
what his relationship was to Chase either, so I just
labeled him a friend when he very well could have
been a family member. I assumed he had money
because that was the point of selling drugs, right? I
didn't think he would go along with it when I invited
him to the club. Shit, I wasn't sure I would go along
with it. For whatever reason, I was feeling kind of
uneasy about it, knowing he was in my city and not
really knowing what he was capable off. Throwing
caution to the wind, I just threw my line into the
ocean and hoped I pulled in the big fish. We'd just
have to see how it went.

When I first got to the club, we were surprisingly
escorted to VIP. Renee's brother controlled the list,
and when we pulled up, he put us right where we
needed to be. I had to catch myself from salivating
as we made our way through and found seats. The
air on this side was different. I was used to being
on the dance floor twerking with the best of them.
These people just sat around and took selfies and
played games on their damn phone. This shit was
dry, but Renee and the crew seemed to be enjoying

themselves as they helped themselves to whatever drink was rotating in the area at the time. Shortly after we got there, there was a little commotion in the area as some guy came in with his squad. He had to be someone important, because the DJ shouted him out immediately upon arrival.

Just out of curiosity, I texted Goon to see if he indeed came to the club. I never put the two together that the NBA star who was just announced and Goon were the same damn person. They definitely didn't call him Goon and definitely said the number from his jersey. I Googled the shit right fast to see who the hell they were talking about, because I couldn't see the guy's face from where I was sitting. He was definitely the man on the court.

As the crowd died down, I decided to see if my project had arrived. I played too damn much, and I knew it. One day it was going to get me killed, but for tonight, I was going to live in the moment.

So you the real deal, huh?

I texted it out to see what his reply would be. I was playing with his mind to see what he thought I knew about him. I didn't know who I was looking for, but he didn't know that, and I just set my sights on the most important guy in the room at the moment. I wanted him to think I had him in the bag and wasn't actually chasing a ghost in the dark. When I saw Mr. NBA reach for his phone, I almost lost it. It was a possibility that he was receiving a text at the same time I was texting him, but his body language said it all.

I just hit the fucking jackpot!

I had to contain myself. I didn't want Renee and them to know what the fuck I had going on, and I didn't want Goon to know I was in such close proximity. When he didn't respond, I sent another text just for good measure to ensure I wasn't getting all hype and dumb for nothing.

Oh, you're shy. It's okay. I'm glad you were able to come out.

I held my breath to see if he would reach for his phone again, and he did. *Oh, my fucking goodness! This shit just changed the damn game!* Here I was thinking I was dealing with some regular schmegular from down the way, and here this fucking millionaire comes making my pussy twitch. He was definitely willing to pay top dollar for any information I had on his friend. I'd bet my $2 million that Selah just gave me on that. He would definitely pay more than that bullshit "wanted" campaign that Selah put out knowing damn well no one would call it in. She already made me a millionaire. I didn't need her anymore, literally or physically. Once I gave this dude the info they needed to move, his crew would have her in the basement just like we had Sajdah, bloody and smelling like her own shit.

I was giddy like a kid on Christmas morning who got everything she asked for. Just like that, Selah be-

came the enemy, and I wasn't too far removed to put
Skye on the list as well. Fuck both them hoes. At the
end of it all, we came in this bitch alone, and we died
alone, unless you were an identical twin and your sister killed you.

All of a sudden, the music felt extra good to
my body, and I had to get up and dance. Turning the
phone completely off, I sensed they usually didn't
dance in VIP, so I skipped my happy ass right to
the dance floor, making sure to lock eyes with Goon.
The women in VIP gave me the craziest look like
they couldn't believe I was passing up the opportunity. I already had money, and if shit went my way, I
was about to get more, so I wasn't worried. I briefly
wondered if he made the connection or if he thought
I was just a pretty face. It didn't matter. If he didn't
know me tonight, he would get to know me sooner
than he thought.

I danced by myself through the first song, and
pretty soon Renee and her girls joined me on the
dance floor. We were too ratchet for VIP, and I didn't
know why we even went up there. I gave Goon a show
for sure, and aside from the money, I didn't have a
problem dropping this WAP in his ass for a pretty
penny. This shit was too good to be true, but I had to
set some shit in motion. I didn't know how long he
was going to be here, so I had to act fast.

I had to get with Skye's ass, too. She wasn't ex-
empt from this wrath. She was on the same type of

time that Selah was on, so I'd just have to show both them bitches. Unfortunately, I'd have to use Renee, but she'd do anything for a damn dollar, so I was sure it wouldn't take too much convincing. It wouldn't even be a top-dollar service, which made it even better. This bitch thought we were best friends. That shit was hilarious to me, but since she wanted to be my friend, I'd just have to see how far she was willing to go for the friendship.

I let the music take over my body and just lived in the moment. It was time I rose to the top and took my rightful place as queen in these streets. My crown had been tilted for way too long, but don't worry. I was fitna get this thing back on straight. People don't always appreciate what you bring to the friendship, and that was okay. It's easier to sit in pain. Imagine sitting in self-love though. You will never underestimate yourself again.

For me, getting revenge always made me feel better, and since Skye and Selah didn't want to be my friend anymore, they would now get the displeasure of seeing what it was like to be my enemy. I wasn't the one you crossed. Especially when I'd laid down my life for you on more than one occasion without question. I'd been saying it from the beginning. Get you a bitch like me on your squad. I would go to the end for you, every single time, without hesitation. I'd put my pussy on the line for her, and she didn't even appreciate it. The nerve.

And Skye's "never choosing a side, always in the middle, couldn't pick a side"–ass . . . Gosh, she made me sick! Fence-riding-ass bitch. She never spoke up, always riding the damn wave. I always hated that about her, but I had something for her ass too. Did I give a damn that her boyfriend just got murdered? Nope. She had made a few bitches feel just like how she felt now, so what goes around comes back around and knocks the shit out of you. She'd be fine, but not until I was done with her ass.

The DJ was playing banger after banger, and I was fucking it up on the dance floor until the lights came up. I no longer saw the guy they called Goon, but it was cool. Now that I knew who he was, I knew how to move. *Ready or not, here I come!* I hoped he was ready for the ride!

Chapter 19

Selah

Going Back In

Seeing the strength that Skye had gave me the courage to pull it together. I couldn't keep living like a damn hermit. This shit wasn't healthy. I decided if I wasn't going to turn myself in for the murders, I might as well get on with my life. I couldn't bring them back, so why keep sitting in this funk? I was still very remorseful, believe me. Don't mistake this newfound vibe for me not caring. This shit was killing me mentally, but I was going to be dead physically if I didn't pull it together soon. I refused to be in a mental institution high on drugs in a padded room, banging my damn head against a wall. I had to get on with life and get my shit together. It was time to make moves.

For the first time in months, I felt different when I got up this morning. For the first time in months, I actually slept through the night without any disturbance from Chance and Sajdah. For the first time in months, I was ready to start living again. I had a lot of catching up to do. When I looked at my bank account this morning, I couldn't believe the amount of money I had in there. I was still working all this time but not spending the money. I had stacked up a pretty penny over the last few months. I felt it was time to start making moves and put this money to use.

I had to get my mom out of her funk as well. I had to handle her with kid gloves though. She was fragile. She lost her daughter. She deserved to live again too. Once I got myself together, I called my therapist to see if he could fit my mom in as well for a quick group session. Maybe if I helped her take the first step, she wouldn't be so reluctant to go. I didn't know what it was about black people and therapy, but we needed it more than anybody else. Our entire existence has been a mess for generations. It was time we became vocal about our shit. We were hurting, and we needed to get it out.

My therapist agreed to see her, so my next step was to get her downtown somehow. Every time we went out, she thought we were going shopping or to eat. That was all she ever wanted to do. This time it was for her healing. I could smell breakfast cooking and could only imagine how much food she had whipped up. I finally, as of late, got her to stop setting a place for Sajdah. I couldn't stop her from cooking up a storm though, so my dad and I decided to let her have that.

"Hey, Ma," I greeted my mom, kissing her and then my dad on the cheek.

"Hey, baby," my mom responded, setting a packed plate in front of me. There was no way I could eat all of this, but I'd definitely give it a go. This meal was definitely going to be delicious. Everything she touched was.

"Hey, baby. How are you feeling?" my dad asked, always concerned about us. He had to be the sweetest soul walking the planet. A real family man. If he ever did some fuck shit to my mom, I promise she did a great job hiding it. For as long as I could remember, he always put us first. Today was no different.

"I'm trying to move forward." I was trying to think of a clever way to get my mom out of the house today, but I couldn't really come up with anything. She was very picky about her outside activities, and I had to word this shit carefully.

"Ma, can you come with me today to some appointments? I could really use some support today."

"Yes, baby. What's wrong? Is your health okay?" she asked, stopping mid-pour of a second cup of coffee for my dad. I hated to have her concerned, but I didn't have a choice.

"Yes, Mommy. I just need a shoulder today."

"Okay, no problem. What time are we heading out? Do I have time to stop in HomeGoods? I saw the cutest throw rug the last time I was there that would be perfect for the basement. Hopefully they still have it. I'm so mad I didn't grab it that day. You know, at stores like that, you have to get it when you see it." She began to ramble as she busied herself cleaning the dishes she had used. It wasn't lost on either Dad or me that she hadn't made herself a plate, but we gave that battle up a long time ago.

"For sure. We don't have to be there until noon. We can go afterward."

I hated to ambush her like this, and I doubted that she would feel like shopping after this meeting. I could only hope that she understood I was trying to protect her heart. She needed this, more than any of us. I'm not saying I needed her to be okay with her child being snatched from her, but I needed her to find some sort of normalcy. I finally got used to hearing her cry at night in my sister's room before going to bed. Hopefully we could get some of those feelings out later today. She didn't do it as much, but the hurt was still there.

I made myself busy in my room trying to decide which business I would like to start. Aside from being severely depressed, I had so many ideas in mind and finally the money to do it. Money: the root of all the damn evil in the world. When I first got the money, I only gave Skye and Vice a couple hundred thousand

apiece. I then doubled back and gave Skye more because I knew she would flip that coin and make it
work. I planned to give her a few more million for
her baby shower gift once we started getting that in
the works. She didn't have any family, so besides her
work family there were really not many people to in-
vite, and I was sure they were giving her a shower at
the gig. I knew Vice would blow through her shit, and
she didn't prove me wrong. I eventually just gave her
a lump sum to shut her up, but I wasn't slow. Vice
had some other shit up her sleeve. That one I would
be watching out for. She was a wild card you could
never be too careful with.

What did I want to do with myself? I wanted to get
away, but guilt wouldn't allow me to leave my parents
in such a fragile state. Once I got them together, I was
out! I was already looking at real estate down South.
Fuck Philly. Love didn't live here anymore.

The closer it got to get ready to go, the tighter my
stomach got. What if she straight snapped on my ass
in this place? Lord, I wasn't ready, and she was so
unpredictable. I sent my dad a text to tell him what
I was doing so that he could be prepared to come get
our asses. He agreed it was time, and I had his full
support. My mom wasn't going to go on her own. I
convinced myself this was the push she needed.

She was ready, patiently waiting for me at the door.
She got herself together today, too, not donning her
usual sweats and Crocs. Hair combed, no baseball

cap. Maybe she was ready for a change too. I wasn't about to question it. I hustled to get her in the car just in case she changed her mind on me. She was notorious for doing that at the last minute, and I didn't feel like fighting with her to come along. She didn't know what I had lined up for the day, and I just hoped our first stop went well.

When we got into Center City, I quickly found a parking space, and I took a deep breath as we made our way up to the therapist's office. She hadn't yet questioned it, and I wasn't about to start no unnecessary shit. She'd know what it was once we got to the back. She took a seat as I checked us in, and it wasn't long before we were ushered to the back. My heart was pounding so hard in my chest I couldn't hear. It felt like the world went silent, and all I could hear was our footsteps sounding like sasquatch feet as we walk down the suddenly too damn long hallway to my therapist's office.

When we finally got to our seats, I felt so exhausted. I didn't know what this session would bring, but I just hoped it gave my mom what she needed to continue with it after today, even if she didn't see the same therapist. There were several in this practice, and all of them were excellent.

"Selah, I'm so glad you could come today," my therapist started as he looked over previous notes. "Mrs. Gordon, I'm elated that you're here as well."

"Thanks for having us," I replied, finally able to hear my voice. This shit had me stressed the fuck out. Lawd, I was ready for it to be over already, and we just got here.

"So just to get us all on the same page, Mrs. Gordon, what we do here is not your stereotypical 'lie on the couch' therapy session. Our goal in helping you heal is doing it the way you want to, at your own pace. We can discuss whatever you want or not. Sometimes people just need to breathe, and this is a safe, non-judgmental space to do so. I'm moving the way you want me to move, okay?"

"So you brought me to a therapist," she stated more than questioned. The look in her eyes belonged to someone I didn't recognize. The anger seemed to simmer and dance on her skin like flames. I fucked up this time, and I didn't know what the hell was going to happen next.

"Mommy, I brought us to a therapist. It's time for us to start healing. We can't stay in this funk forever," I replied, batting back tears. I didn't want to offend her in this process. I knew it would be difficult, but it had to be done.

"You don't get to kill my daughter and tell me when to heal from it."

What?

My entire body came out of itself and went back in. What did she know? Who told her? Did she figure it out on her own? The way my body was starting to shut down had me shaking in my seat. I was speech-less and didn't know what to do.

"Mommy," I began.

"Your sister told me everything, Selah. She won't get out of my dreams. She told me you did this to her," she said with a straight face.

Okay, so she was a fucking loony tune. Well, not really. Sajdah showed up in my dreams often to haunt me too, but this was just too much. Now I was stuck between a rock and a hard place. *Do I deny that shit until the end, or do I risk it all and confirm her suspicions?*

"Okay, let's just take a moment to gather ourselves," my therapist jumped in, sensing shit was about to go all the way left. My heart hurt so bad at this moment. How long had she been feeling this way? Or was some snake feeding her this information, and she just registered it as a dream? Did she tell my dad this shit? Probably not, because he definitely would have said something to me about it. Or would he? His loyalty surely lay with my mom. Those feelings of not trusting anybody were creeping back in, and I couldn't let them win.

"Mrs. Gordon, why do you have these feelings? Why do you feel Selah possibly murdered her sister?" he asked. I turned right to her face because I needed to hear this shit. I had the blackassity to be offended. This was all just too much.

"You know, they always had a little jealous streak with each other. Since they were little," my mom began. "Sajdah wanted to be like Selah so bad, but she could never figure it out," she said with a slight laugh as she reminisced. "The two of them were so much alike that they were completely different, if that makes sense. They had been going through something shortly before Sajdah's passing. Then one day my baby just ended up dead. She came to me in a dream one night, crying, telling me to forgive you, Selah. She told me you didn't mean it, and it was all a misunderstanding."

I was in full-blown tears. Maybe this wasn't the best idea after all. It was all a dream she had. Thankfully it was not solid proof, but I was so scared of what she would do with this information eventually. What if she got fed up and went to the law and they started an investigation? We'd all be fucked. This just reminded me that I needed to either watch those videos and burn the evidence or fuck the videos and just get rid of them now. My curiosity wouldn't let me not know, and I vowed as soon as I got home, no matter how long it took me, I'd be watching until the end.

"Mom, I didn't—"

"Mrs. Gordon," my therapist began in a calm voice. "Sometimes when we dream, it becomes the fruition of wishful thinking. From what I understand about your daughter's passing, it was sudden, and you never really got any answers. It's easy to try to come to a conclusion that you can cope with.

"Now I'm not saying what you experienced in your dream state wasn't real to you, but I want you to be open to the idea that just maybe you are looking for any closure you can get, and since your daughters were so close, just maybe it's easier for you to blame her for what happened. Selah, from what I gather, was Sajdah's protector, and this one time she wasn't able to be. Your dreams are valid, and I think moving forward we should look deeper into your perception. However, it's unfair to place blame without facts. Sometimes grief gets us stuck, and we don't know how to move, so we look for any answer we can find, even if it doesn't make sense. Can we agree to that?"

She sat in silence staring at the therapist without blinking for what felt like an eternity. Meanwhile, my entire world was crumbling around me, and it felt like I was in the middle of the room trying to keep the ceiling from crushing me. My lungs felt tight, and I took small sips of air to try to push my way through. *This pain* . . . My mom hated me.

Just when I thought I couldn't take another minute, she burst into tears that seemed to come from her toes. The wails that escaped her throat were so sharp and fierce it was like knives slicing me like paper cuts just on the surface followed up by alcohol in the open wounds. I needed my dad. This was not a good idea.

I didn't know what I was supposed to do, but I reached over anyway and took her into my arms. Her cry vibrated through my entire body, but I didn't let her go. As much as this shit killed me, I held her like I'd never get to again.

I held her until her tears subsided and she could catch her breath. When she finally gathered herself, she looked me in the eyes, and I struggled to not look away. I didn't want her to see the truth in my eyes. I didn't want her to confirm her suspicions in my face, but I held our gaze because my life depended on it.

"Selah, I'm sorry. I'm glad you brought me here, and I can see that I need to be here. The dreams just seemed so real." She looked down at her hands then looked back at me. "I don't know where my mind is these days, but I appreciate your efforts, and I'm ready to start healing. I love you. I really do."

I just sat quietly. This was a bit much, even for me. I sat quietly as the therapist and my mom continued their conversation, and once she made an appointment with one of his colleagues, we were finally ready to go. My body was still vibrating from this ordeal, and there wasn't a soul I could talk to about it. *Lord, have mercy on my soul!*

As he escorted us out, he asked me to stay back for a second while my mom got situated with her soon-to-be therapist up front. That shit hit heavy when it was the truth, and I just didn't know what space to be in at the moment.

"You okay?" he asked, offering me a tissue as a fresh stream of tears stained my face. I was at a loss for words. "I know that was hard for you, but it's a part of the healing process. Your mom will come around. Just hang in there. I'm here whenever you need me. Never feel like you don't have someone to talk to, okay? We've made progress, even though for you it may feel like a step back. Let's continue to move forward."

I shook my head like I understood, then made my way up front. She was standing by the elevator with an odd look on her face that I chose to ignore. I was slightly afraid, not knowing if she was going to ambush me again. When we got down to the car, I started making my way toward home. I was practically speeding as I tried to get through the city as quickly as possible to put distance between us and the session.

"I thought we were going to HomeGoods," she said once she realized that the route we were taking led us back to our house. I made a mental note to call my Realtor once I got in. It was time for me to go. I couldn't be in this house anymore knowing how she felt about me, and also knowing her feelings held validity.

"I'll have Daddy take you, Ma. I have another appointment I need to get to."

"Selah, I'm—"

"Ma, it's okay. We're going to be okay."

I reached over to grab her hand, and for the first time she didn't flinch or move to snatch her hand away. That shit scared me even more. When we finally got to the house, my dad was outside waiting for us. I had texted him to give an ETA and told him we needed to talk. He hugged us both, then ushered my mom into his car so that they could go buy more shit she didn't need.

I ran straight up to my room and locked the door behind me. Pulling up the videos, I began watching them slightly fast-forwarded. I didn't need to hear the sounds. I just needed to see who was there. My breath caught in my throat the first time I caught Sajdah on the video. The date definitely read before Chase and I became a thing. Maybe there was some truth in what she told me. I took note of that as I continued to watch. I was sure seeing her wouldn't be my only surprise, and I vowed whatever I saw would be handled accordingly.

Chapter 20

Momma Gordon

Sometimes You Just Have to Say It

Whew! It felt good getting that out. Let me be the first to tell you that I never wanted to hurt my baby. Selah was the last of my children, and I felt like at this point we should be as close as possible. We only had each other left. Me, her, and her father. I never thought the day would come that I'd have to bury another one of my children, but it happened, and it shifted my spirit, and not in a good way. I didn't have solid proof, but she had something to do with her sister's demise. I wasn't exactly sure how, but baby girl wasn't innocent in this matter. I'd put my life on it and double down.

When we had the twins, the feeling I got from that couldn't be put into words. We prayed for them.

We had a few failed pregnancies before they came along and were very hopeful that this last round of in vitro fertilization would work. I suffered from cystic fibrosis, which made it hard for me to get pregnant and maintain pregnancy. People think this mess is easy. For many people, they can just sit next to a penis and end up pregnant. For just as many others, it's an exhausting and emotional roller coaster that for so many still doesn't produce fruit. We spent so much money on the process, and I just felt like this time was the one.

And it was. We got double the blessing. As happy as I was, an entirely new set of stress set in. See, getting pregnant is a small part of the battle. Once that happens, you have to try to hold this baby in your body for nine months. Or, in my case with the twins, preferably up to thirty-eight weeks. Let me tell you how I was a salad-eating, water-drinking, organic-everything type of mom-to-be taking every class that was offered. I didn't want to mess this up, but I never spoke of the anxiety because I didn't want to alarm my husband. He, as well, was hopeful things would go as planned this time. The grief doesn't just fall on the mother. We both felt the loss each and every time.

God blessed us, and it was just what we needed. Not that our marriage was on the rocks or anything. Our thing was solid. We felt the need to bring it full circle, and for us that was having children of our own.

When I got to look into the faces of these beauties after my cesarean section, I knew my life would be nothing like I knew it moving forward. These beauties were gifted to me, to us, and it was up to me to make sure I did what I was set out to do: protect the gifts at all costs.

Boy, did these girls keep me busy. Sajdah always wanted to read a book to me, and she was smart beyond her years. I knew she would be my scholar. She was more interested in science kits and crunching numbers than playing with dolls. My little genius. She didn't want the typical Halloween costume. Always wanted to be something she learned from school. A train conductor, or historian like Harriet Tubman. Although she came out minutes after her sister, she was the first to do it all. Take steps, grow teeth, call me Momma. That one I knew I didn't have to worry about. She took life by the horns at an early age and never looked back.

Selah was, well, she was different, to say the least. Although she marched to the beat of her own drum also, her beat had a little more bop in it than usual, as the young ones would say. She had some sass on her. She knew she was pretty early on and used that to get what she wanted plenty of times. Those eyes always got you. She was my little fashionista, and Sajdah just couldn't keep up.

They were joined at the hip until, against my better judgment, I was forced to separate them in school.

Let them be individuals, they said. They can't be stuck together forever, they need to find out who they are, they warned me. I should have stuck to my guns and fought for them to stay together. That was when I began to see their individuality, and it was scary. What I thought I could keep together slowly began to drift apart right in front of my eyes, and it scared me. Having a twin is like having a built-in best friend, and I never wanted my girls to lose sight of that.

We tried for one more, be it another set of twins or an individual child. It took years again to get that one, and once again just when we thought to give up, we were pregnant with another, our final child. Scared the hell out of me, but I was ready. From the moment I heard the heartbeat, I was in love. Our little family was growing, and I couldn't be prouder of what we had accomplished. I was moving right along with this pregnancy. Not nearly as many complications as when I was carrying the twins. At the eighteen-week mark, I found out I was having a boy, and I couldn't believe we were being blessed like this again.

That day, I went home and began decorating the room to be fit for a little prince. I mean, I literally left the doctor's office and went right to several baby stores to get started. I wanted to tell the twins what was going on also. I mean, they were old enough to obviously see that I was pregnant, but a conversation was in order because I didn't know what that meant to them. I set up the room with what I had with plans to get more stuff later in the week.

Four days later, before I could even get back to the store, a sharp pain ripped through my body that felt so hot it took my breath away. I tried getting up to go to the restroom, and for whatever reason I couldn't feel my legs from the waist down. I was able to flip the lamp on in the room, fear gripping me and squeezing my throat. I felt this feeling before with other miscarriages. I was so far along this time. Surely I was out of the danger zone.

I tried to quietly maneuver without alerting my husband, who was sound asleep next to me. I swear this man could sleep through anything. When I finally got the nerve to pull the covers back, the scream that came from my throat probably woke the entire neighborhood. There was so much blood, more than I'd ever seen in my life. My husband jumped into action immediately.

All I remembered was him scooping me from the bed and carrying me down the steps as my neighbor went upstairs to be with our girls. I didn't remember the car ride over or them ripping my stillborn baby from my gut while I was passed out. I had lost so much blood I went into shock and had to have a blood transfusion to bring me back. When I finally opened my eyes, it was a few days later. My husband's eyes were bloodshot, probably from crying. My stomach was almost back flat as if I'd never been pregnant at all.

When the doctors came in, they all sounded like
Charlie Brown's teacher after they told me my son
hadn't survived. The doctor called it APS, antiphos-
pholipid syndrome. Simply put, my body formed a
blood clot in the placenta, and that cut off his oxygen,
causing preeclampsia. With all of the issues with
getting pregnant prior, it was a wonder that I wasn't
tested for this earlier. I felt so empty when I finally
returned home without my son.

Oh, the tears I cried. I felt like such a failure. My
husband tried his best to console me, but it had to
run its course. The feeling of grief again. The feeling
like a failure again. The disbelief again. For me, it was
really the not having my baby again. Our girls were
at their aunt's house having a ball with their cousins.
My sister called to check in daily and told me not to
worry about them. They had questions of course, but
they were just fine. It was like a never-ending slum-
ber party for them. By the time they got back home,
our son's room was completely packed up and gone.
It was painted and decorated for Sajdah. I still didn't
agree that they should be separated, but I didn't want
the stress of trying to fill the room with another child
again. I made an appointment with my gynecologist
and got my tubes tied shortly after. I couldn't do this
again, and the girls would be enough for me from
now on.

I knew my kids. I knew when they weren't shooting straight with me. I began to worry about them

months prior to Sajdah's murder, because let's face it—that was what the hell it was. They weren't as tight as they used to be. I used to stand outside of the door and listen to their conversations, and that was the first thing I noticed. Those talks became few and far between.

Yes, they were both now adults and living in their own worlds, but these two, even in their own worlds, rotated around each other like the moon and the sun rotated around the earth. Something wasn't right with my babies, and when Selah came to me about it, it killed me on the inside. The day had come when they were growing up and didn't depend on each other as much anymore. Seeing my oldest twin like that sat down in my gut and twisted like a tornado. I couldn't keep saving them, though. I had to let them figure this out on their own.

Those two started moving like thieves in the night, seemingly purposely avoiding each other. Selah eventually moved out, I believed to take some of the heat off of whatever they were going through. Again, I wanted to intervene, but my husband told me to mind my business. Why did I listen to him? I should have followed my gut and tried to get my girls back together, but I didn't. I should have, and I didn't, and it was killing me. I made sure to speak with them daily because I could see the kind of pain they were both in. I just wish I knew what it was about.

I didn't pry.

I should have.

I should have pulled their asses together and made them hash it out.

One day I called Sajdah, and her phone went right to voicemail. I couldn't remember a time ever that I couldn't reach either one of them. I called Selah, and her phone rang but she didn't answer. I figured maybe Sajdah had forgotten to charge her phone. Something she never did, but there's a first time for everything, right? Later in the day when she still hadn't called, I called Selah back to inquire. She said she hadn't heard from her either, but the way she said it just didn't sit right with me. She didn't sound concerned at all. Yeah, they were mad at each other for God knows what reason, but still. She actually kind of rushed me off the phone, but I let it slide because I was too busy trying to find my other baby.

Their dad tried to get me to calm down, but my soul was uneasy. Coincidentally her place of employment did a wellness check because she hadn't shown up for work in a few days. By the third day when she hadn't called or come home, I went right down to the police station to file the report. I didn't tell anyone I was doing it because I didn't want to hear that I was overreacting. I just did what I had to do to find my youngest twin, and if that meant looking crazy in these streets, then that's what it was.

Can I just tell you that when the call came in a few days later from the hospital saying that a body had been found, and it may be Sajdah, every breath I had left in my body evaporated into thin air? The man explained that it was a possibility that it wasn't her, but she fit the description of the female I reported missing. I would have to come down to the hospital to identify the body they had found abandoned in the projects. A few families were called who had reports on missing females, so it was likely we wouldn't be the only family there. My daughters didn't hang in the damn projects, or did they? I'd like to think they had more class than that, but the one friend Selah had was definitely a hood rat, so I wouldn't be too surprised.

I didn't go to the hospital. I couldn't. Literally, for the second time in my life, my legs stopped working and I couldn't move. My neighbor came and sat with me while my husband and my daughter went to the hospital. It felt like an eternity as I waited for them to call me and tell me that it wasn't her. My hand gripped the phone so tight my knuckles had turned white. My breath was gone. I had no idea how I was living at the moment. She was my right lung, Selah my left. Their deceased siblings and every child from every miscarriage lived in my heart. I needed them all to survive.

The phone rang.

Everything after that moved in slow motion as my neighbor held my crumpled body like a newborn child, wiping her tears in the process. Our babies grew up together. Her son was murdered three years prior. She knew exactly what this feeling was. The shock. The terror. The disbelief. My baby was snatched from me, and I couldn't understand why.

By this time, Selah had already moved back home the week before. I guessed she and her little boyfriend didn't work out, but still there was something odd about the way she moved now. I knew my babies. Her flow was different, and I couldn't quite put my finger on it. By the time Sajdah's memorial service came, I could barely make it through. We had no choice but to cremate due to what was done to her body in death. This wasn't how it was supposed to go, but here we were again. Her urn was smaller than her brother's casket ages before.

Selah was right by my side, the way she should be. She did everything she could to help find her sister's killers and all that. The reward setup, the flyers, the constant check on the investigation. She did it all. Yet something just wasn't sitting right with it for me. She looked more guilty than anything, and when I slid that info past my husband, he dismissed it immediately.

"You think she did it?" I asked him one night as we watched *Jeopardy!* He looked at me like I was crazy.

"How could you think that she did?" he asked, waiting for an answer.

I couldn't run the risk of telling him that Sajdah came to me in my dream the night that she died. She cried for me to help her, and I couldn't do anything to help her. I knew she was gone, and I was just waiting for confirmation.

"Our daughter is not a murderer. Especially not her sister's," he explained for what felt to him like the hundredth time even though this was only my first time bringing it up. "They went through something, yes, but not something that would make them bring harm or death to each other. I know you want answers, but that's not it."

From that moment on I kept the thoughts to myself, but I watched her like a hawk. Something wasn't right, and I would find out why if it killed me, or I killed her. I would see the therapist. It wouldn't hurt to get some of this shit out of my head, but just know that Sajdah Gordon's death would not be in vain. Even if that meant taking out my own child for it.

Chapter 21

Skye

Philly Curvy, Est. 2020

By the time my child's father was laid to rest, I was better able to deal with his demise. His family was an entire mess, but we got through it. His sister was really cool, and I ended up offering her a job at my store once it was all said and done. His mom wanted to fight me and told me more than once that she didn't because her grandchild was in my stomach, but it was on sight as soon as the baby popped out of my pussy. It was beyond me why she thought this shit was my fault, but I just gave it to her. I wasn't about to argue with a bunch of strangers about something I had no control over. Shit, it ain't like I was the one who killed him. If I knew who did it, I'd already be on their ass, but I digress. He would want me to keep moving forward, and that was what I would do.

In his memory, once the baby was born, I'd tattoo his name on my rib because he was always by my side.

I pushed the date back a little, but finally 90 percent of my inventory was in, and I felt I had enough to get set up and open. Everything didn't need to be out all at once. I had to keep telling myself that. I didn't want the store to look cluttered, but I didn't want it to look empty. I brought Renee on as my manager, and she gladly accepted the position. Out of all the people I got the chance to interview prior to my situation, she definitely showed up and showed out. I didn't get a chance to interview as many applicants as I wanted to, but I had enough people to start so I just gave them all a job based on their skill level, minus the two who had the worst attitudes ever.

Renee came in and got right to work. Her fashion sense was sick, and the color combinations she pulled together on these mannequins had me like, *wow!* She knew her shit, and I just kind of gave her free reign as she directed the other nine people I had hired to get the store together. I had a four-teen-day window to get the store up and running so that we could start making this bread. I had already been paying rent on this spot for a few months, and I needed to recoup those funds ASAP. I had a layout for the store in mind, but she came in and put this place right where I needed it to be. I knew I made a good choice in hiring her. I just hoped once everything got rolling, she'd keep up the momentum.

I had also been looking at houses. I was ready to go. Philly just wasn't doing it for me anymore, and I needed a change of scenery. I wasn't necessarily opposed to living in the country. Havertown was far enough away to be isolated but close enough to still handle and grow my business. I couldn't go too far with the store just opening, but I couldn't stay in this house for much longer. I couldn't breathe in here. I needed a do-over.

The days seemed to zip past as we got closer to the grand opening. Renee had secured the DJ, models, extra security, and food for the event. She even had the models' looks already picked out by model type. I had already sent the invitations out personally to Vice and Selah, and I had the team working social media to get the buzz going. I could feel this was going to be a good start to my business, and any doubt that tried to come in, I simply prayed away. When my grandmother was alive, she would always tell me that you can't plant the seed and keep digging it up to see if it sprouted. Just keep it watered and watch it grow. We worked diligently until the store was ready to go, and I was really proud of us. Right before my eyes, it was all coming together better than I could have imagined. Not too many hiccups, and everyone was co-operating. Finally, I felt like God was giving me the break I needed. I'd done some bad shit to people over the years, but I never stopped praying for forgiveness. I thought He finally heard me.

Renee was serious about this shit. She had some really cute ideas, and I let her convince me into turning the middle of the store, just for the grand opening, into a runway. By the time she was done, I was considering keeping it that way. The layout was flawless. She had real runway staging with crystal chairs lined up for people to watch the show. The red carpet and gold rope gave it an official catwalk look. I mean, she had lighting set up, and she had the models practicing after-hours to make sure they had their walk together. I was getting so giddy with excitement as I watched it all come together as the days went by, and I welcomed the distraction of not thinking about my son's father. It was more difficult when I was home by myself, so I needed this distraction.

I had already secured the licensing I needed to serve liquor for the event, and my caterer was not to be played with. Soul-food eggrolls, fried mac-and-cheese balls, sweet-chili meatballs—man, I couldn't wait to make my plate! When I arrived at the store opening day morning, I was blown away by what she had accomplished. This shit brought me to tears. I couldn't believe it was finally happening. The Fashion District had never seen this kind of flavor, and I couldn't wait to be the talk of the city. Having to follow up behind Milano, Banni Peru, The Sable Collective, and Expect Lace was no easy task, but I was up for the challenge. I was about to put us curvy sistas on that splah! We liked to look well put together, too, and I felt like the line I had in mind would be well received.

Donned in one of the maternity pieces that I offered in the store, I showed up runway ready, baby bump on full display. She had a cute red carpet set up outside of the store and everything, complete with balloons, and even a Hollywood star sat by the carpet for people to take pics by. I didn't know where she found time to do all of this on such short notice, but she definitely worked her magic, and I was pleased beyond measure. The day was mostly a blur. People showed up and showed out as the ding from the cash register seemed to go nonstop all day long. I got an amazing picture with Selah and a few other friends I had from down the way. People shopped, enjoyed the food and drink, and had an all-around good time. To my surprise, she even got news coverage for the event that brought even more people to the location. She showed out! I was proud of her and the entire team.

My fashionistas stocked the store throughout the day as items sold, and for items that sold out, we took orders to ship them at a later date. This was such a blessing. I was happy we were able to pull it off, but it made me so sad that my man couldn't be here with me to celebrate this. He was definitely here in spirit, and I did my best to hold my tears in check as I took pic after pic throughout the day, creating memories.

By late afternoon I was exhausted but still rolling. This baby was kicking the hell out of me to the beat of the music, and it didn't feel good, but I kept it pushing. Selah helped around the store, but it didn't go unnoticed that Vice had yet to show her raggedy ass up in here. I promise you will always find out who your real friends are when you have something important happening. I wasn't totally shocked. We had been in a rough place lately, but surely you can put all of that to the side for a few hours to celebrate with your best friend, right? I'd be lying if I said my feelings weren't hurt. I definitely felt some type of way, and I would definitely be letting her know. This shit had to end. We were better than this. Or at least I thought we were. I'd find out as soon as I caught up with her.

As I was helping check out customers, I noticed a little crowd forming outside the store, and I was nervous that a fight was about to break out. Pretty soon the people in the store all began to gather outside, including my staff. I watched from the register because I didn't have another step left in my body to be nosy. My feet were already swollen more than usual from all the standing I'd been doing today. The photographer flicked it up as I noticed a gentleman outside signing autographs and taking pics. Clearly, he was someone important. I just didn't know who he was.

"Skye, you need to get your wobble on and come take some pics, ma. It's not every day an NBA star shows up to shop at your store," Renee suggested as she quickly got back outside. Selah took control of the register as I made my way out front.

"Let's give it up for the owner of this boutique, Skye!" Renee announced me to the crowd as I came out. Loud applause erupted as I smiled and thanked everyone for coming, and I eventually made it over to Mr. NBA. I wasn't a basketball person, so I still had no clue who he was. Right before I got close to him, I spied Vice's rusty ass standing by the Piercing Pagoda kiosk. *Why didn't she come inside and say something to me or Selah? I'm sure she saw us in there.*

"He's number seventeen on the Miami Heat. They just won the championship," Renee spoke into my ear as best she could as she escorted me up front. When I got to him, he took my hand and pulled me over for the photo. We took a few pics, and then we made our way into the store.

"This is very nice what you have going on here," he began as he looked around. "I heard about it on the news, so I decided to come down and get some stuff for my fiancée. Give me everything you have in a size twelve. Every shoe in a size nine. Be sure to throw some bling in there, too."

Renee got right on it as she directed the girls to start scouring the racks and the inventory in the back of what we had left in the size he requested. He and I continued to converse as she prepared the packages for him and began to tally up the cost. He didn't even bother to check the total as he simply handed over his Amex, and we continued to talk. He had a few guys blocking the door so it was just us in the store.

"Thank you so much for the support," I responded as Renee took about ten bags of clothing, accessories, and shoes to the door for him.

"Anytime. I wish my boy had gone in this direction, but his dreams were cut short. He could have had a spot just like this in this very mall."

"Oh, who's your friend? Philly is small. I may know him," I quizzed just for the sake of conversation. You never know who knows who in the world. I'd been clear across the country at times and had seen people from down the way. You never know who you'll run into.

"He's no longer with us, but his name is . . . was Chase. He talked about having a clothing store often," he said, looking nostalgic.

Thank God I was good at keeping my poker face. The way my body froze instantly gave me goose bumps. If this was who I thought it was, he would not be happy to know who I turned out to be.

"I appreciate your time," he continued. "Maybe we can collaborate on something in the future. I've always wanted a clothing line and would love to open a flagship store in the city where I'm from."

"Absolutely. I'll definitely be in touch," I said as I took his card, trying to keep my hands from shaking. I almost threw up on his shoes. That was how nervous I got. He was standing in the same room as the murderer and the girl who helped bury the evidence, and he didn't even know it. This was just too much at one time.

Once he was gone, I ran to the back, grabbing Selah on the way and making sure the door was locked before talking. I felt like I was going to vomit all over everything. Did he know who I was? Of course he didn't, I tried to convince myself. Would he spend money with someone responsible for his friend's demise? I had to take a seat before I fucked around and passed out back here. I couldn't afford another trip to the hospital.

"What's wrong?" Selah asked as she kneeled beside me, concerned.

"Do you know who that was?"

"I don't, but he appears to have a lot of money. Everyone kept saying he was a basketball player."

"Not just any basketball player," I began, almost in tears. "I believe that is Chase's friend from Miami."

"Goon?" she asked. "Chase had been trying to get me to go meet him, but I never made the time. I casually conversed with him on a FaceTime once, but I couldn't put a face to the name. If he walked up to me right now, I wouldn't know who he was."

"He gave me this card." I pulled it out and showed it to her. The name on the card didn't ring a bell, but just maybe we could use it to our advantage still. "He said he was interested in working with me. His friend

Chase wanted to open a clothing store, but he was no longer with us. Who the fuck else could he be talking about?"

She sat down and had the same look I did. Did he know us? We hoped he didn't. What the hell were we going to do if he did? Unable to hold it in anymore, I ran to the restroom to vomit. I didn't know what to do or what to think. We needed Vice here. When I came back in, Selah had a strange look on her face. She clearly had something to say, but I just couldn't take any more bad news.

"Well, sis, that's not our only issue. Sajdah wasn't the only one sneaking and fucking Chase."

"What?" I damn near screamed as I made my way over to her. "What do you mean?"

"Well, I was going to talk to you about this another day because I didn't want to ruin your opening for you," she began, teary-eyed. "A lot happened a few weeks ago when I took my mom to therapy with me. That's a story for another day. Anyhoo, when I got home, I sat and watched the videos from Chase's surveillancc. I have a feeling Vice knew about Sajdah well before I did and played me against my sister. I'm not just talking about the photos she produced. There's more to it than that. After all, she had been to Chase's more than I wanted to count. He had surveillance inside the house. I saw everything."

My heart broke for my friend. I knew she wasn't ready to know the entire truth. I had no idea Vice was ever seeing Chase aside of the few chance meetings she told me about. She went above and beyond to place the blame on Sajdah when she was just as guilty all this time. That shit had me on fire like you wouldn't believe, and I wanted to go get her ass now. I hated a wolf in friend's clothing.

"Selah, I'm so sorry."

"No need to be. I'll fix her. Don't even mention it to her. We will just move like usual until the time comes. We will talk again. Now straighten yourself up," she said to me as she wiped my face and tossed me a lip balm from my inventory. "We have to get through this grand opening. I'm proud of you, and I love you, friend. Now let's go get the rest of this money."

As we came from the back, I was surprised again by a beautiful cake from my favorite baker, It's Buttercream, Baby! in West Philly. I promise she had the best cakes in the city. The cake was carved into a mannequin wearing one of the outfits I sold in the store. It was hard, but I faked the smile as tears ran down my face. I was sure everyone thought they were happy tears, but I was steaming mad on the inside. I smiled for the pictures though and accepted Vice's hug and well-wishes as the party began to wrap up. I gave Renee instructions on how to close for the day as Selah and I made our way out. We had to talk more, and this wasn't the place to do it.

"I just want to thank all of you for coming out," I spoke to the people who were still shopping. "My staff brought this together in less than two weeks. I couldn't ask for better employees. Renee, from the moment you came in and turned that mannequin out, I knew you were the one. I appreciate you. She made all of this happen, y'all," I shouted, joining in on the applause. "Thank you all for everything. And be sure to come back and shop some more."

A laugh spread across the room, and I hugged as many people as I could as I inched toward the door. This was a bittersweet moment for me. I didn't miss Vice's stank look that she was giving from the sideline, but I'd deal with her another time.

"He spent twenty-five thousand, sis!" Renee informed me as she helped direct the rest of the employees.

She definitely charged his ass up. I didn't have that much shit in a twelve for it to cost that much, but whatever. I'd be sure she got a commission for the sale.

"I'll have everything recorded for you and all receipts gathered by morning. Here is the drop for the day to take to the bank. The rest can go tomorrow. I don't feel comfortable with this kind of money on the premises."

Loyalty. This further confirmed that I could trust her, at least for now. I also had access to the software, and there was surveillance all over the store from every angle, so I could always backtrack to see what was what for the day. I thanked her for her time, and we rolled out.

I sat in silence as we first made the drop at the bank then went to my house. I had to remember I was pregnant, because I was ready to cause some damage. We pulled up to my house shortly and made our way inside. After I set my things down and got comfortable, I turned to my friend since grade school and caught the hurt on her face. This time I wasn't willing to let it slide.

"So," I began as I hugged my belly, "how are we gonna get this bitch?"

Chapter 22

Goon

Putting a Face to the Name

You just all over the city, huh?

My phone buzzed, indicating I had a text while I was down at the Fashion District the other day. I read the text and left it there. I was not about to let home-girl think she had me in the bag. I already decided that no matter what information she gave me, I was going to kill her. Okay, maybe not me personally, but she was definitely a done bun. My boys refused to let me get my hands dirty, so the hit was out. I just had to put a face to the name.

Speaking of faces, I saw the twin at the event while I was there. Based on a pic one of the crew showed me, she looked just like the girl I saw on FaceTime once while speaking with Chase. I just didn't know which one she was. None of us did. I wasn't the type to just be taking people out all willy-nilly. I had to make sure we had the right one. My team would clear the entire fucking neighborhood out, no questions asked. All I had to do was say the word, but I didn't want that blood on my hands. Philly had enough senseless death happening. I wasn't about to contribute to it. I'd just get my intended target and bounce.

When I got the text yesterday, I definitely noticed it didn't come from her. My eyes were on her the entire time she was helping in the store. I also saw the one I was talking to grab her and go to the back, so she wasn't the one either. I briefly scanned the crowd to see if anyone was acting suspect, but everyone was too busy shopping and enjoying the moment. The question was, what did they know about my boy? I was genuine when I said I wanted to work with her on opening a store. She could be the sister store to my brand. I also had other questions, and I hoped that she called me before I left town. Whoever it was had the drop on me, and I didn't like it. My constant jumping at my phone gave her control over me that I wasn't willing to relinquish. I had to find a way to flip this around.

Shorty with the freckles though, this wasn't my first time seeing her. I also saw her at the gas station the other night. She didn't look like she recognized me, but who knew? She got her gas and dipped before I could get to her. When I saw the camera pan on her at the event, I immediately made my way to

Center City to see if I could catch her. I wanted to say something to her there, but there were so many people, I couldn't get to her to talk privately. Then when the people realized who I was, it was a wrap. I had to pull out the Amex and support. I was relieved to see that the boutique owner was her friend, so now I thought I had a way in.

It didn't take her long to call, surprisingly. She called the next day to set up a meeting. This was perfect because I only had three more days before my flight, and I was really hoping to get some traction before I left. She seemed eager to talk business, and I decided to meet her at her store so that we could possibly get a collab going. Mystery Girl was blowing my phone up all of a sudden, and I could tell she was getting upset that I wasn't responding. She was losing her grip on the situation, and it was looking like the tables were starting to turn. I still needed her, but she didn't need to know that. Besides, the minute I no longer needed her she'd be put out with the trash. Take that any way you wish.

I arrived at the store a little before my scheduled time just to see how business was going after the grand opening earlier in the week. Surprisingly it was just as packed today. It could be because it was new to the District. You know how people be all hype in the beginning. I needed to see what this store was doing a few months from now to know how and if I really wanted to invest in this venture. I was glad that she called me before I left to at least get the ball rolling.

As I watched her move in the store, I spotted the twin in there, too. This was my lucky day! I somehow needed to figure out which one she was. My security lurked not far from me, but they were ready to spray the place at the drop of a hat. All I had to do was give the word. I didn't want to intimidate them with bodyguards and all of that, so I made them stand back and blend in with the other people shopping and enjoying what the food court had to offer. No one wants to do business feeling afraid.

As she was ringing up a customer, I walked into the store and took it all in. She scaled down the runway that was there the previous day, but I still loved what she had done with the place. I could see a few of the women taking advantage of the floor-to-ceiling 360-degree mirrors as they walked the catwalk and admired their potential new outfits before purchasing. What she had set up here was genius, and I could see the esteem boost that this place was offering to the ladies who shopped here. If she kept this up, she could definitely open a few locations in the near future.

When she noticed me standing at the front, she smiled in acknowledgement, putting up a finger letting me know she'd be with me shortly. I gave her a nod, not wanting to disturb her flow. Shortly after, another young lady took control at the register, and she motioned me to the back, grabbing the twin along the way.

She had a nice little swanky setup back here. Nothing like I thought it would be. I thought I was going to walk into a bunch of boxes and chaos, but to my surprise everything was just as organized in the back as the front. The clothes were hanging in moveable closets that looked to be by color. A few mannequins stood fully dressed off to the side, and her office space was immaculate. She was organized and about her business. I liked to see that.

She offered me a seat in front of the desk, and she and the twin were on the other side, her sitting and the twin standing. We just kind of stared at each other in an awkward silence that had me second-guessing being here. Did they know who I was? Did my guards give me away?

"Thank you so much for meeting with us," she began with a smile that put me at ease but not too much. My guard always stayed up just in case I had to punch these bitches and dip. "I really appreciate your support the other day."

"No problem. I love what you have going on here. Like I mentioned before, a good friend of mine was thinking about going in this direction. I'd love to do something in his honor and open a few stores."

I didn't miss the glance they gave each other, but I decided to let them move the conversation in the direction they wanted to go. They were curious, I was sure, to know who I was referring to, but they'd have to ask if they really wanted to know. I wasn't giving out information just because.

"Who is your friend? Seems like you guys were super close. I'm sorry for your loss," the twin said as they both leaned in seemingly for the answer. They were fishing, but I was up for being caught if it gave me the answers I needed.

"His name was Chase," I began, choking back tears as I continued. "He was taken from us a little over a year ago. Did you know him?"

"If it's the same Chase we knew, he was my sister's boyfriend. She was murdered around the same time of his disappearance," the twin answered. I looked her in the eyes to gauge her. The eyes tell you everything you need to know. She was still hurting from her sister's demise. I felt her pain.

"What happened?" I asked, hoping they would give me something to go off of. The pain that covered their faces made me regret asking, but I would regret it even more if I didn't at least try to get an answer. For the first time in months, I finally felt like I was getting somewhere. This shit hits differently when someone else understands your pain.

"We are still trying to figure it out. My sister's body was found in the projects. She and Chase were very close, so we are guessing whoever did this to her must have gotten him too," the boutique owner answered. The twin just looked drained, and I could dig it. I'd been feeling that exact same way for months now, so forgive me if I wasn't all that sympathetic toward her talking about it.

"I offered a reward and everything," the twin chimed in. "Nothing is done in the hood without somebody seeing it. Surprisingly no one has come through yet, but we are not giving up until we get an answer."

I leaned back in the chair and took it all in. I went back and forth on if I was going to tell them about the calls I'd been getting. Shit, ain't like they were the police. What were they going to do to me? Maybe if I told them, they would know who it was. I decided to just toss the shit out there and see where it landed.

"So," I began, clearing my throat and hoping I wasn't making a mistake. "I've been getting calls and texts from Chase's phone. Well, the person who has Chase's phone now has a new number."

"What?" they screamed in unison. This was beginning to be too much, but I was already on the damn edge. *Might as well jump in the deep end.*

"Well, periodically I would call his phone just to hear his voice. I still can't believe my brother is gone. To my surprise, one day someone answered the phone. At first no one said anything, but after a while she—"

"She?" they both responded, cutting me off. The twin looked like she was going to cry, and the pregnant one was slumped down in the chair so far it looked uncomfortable. They were losing it, but we had to get this shit out.

"Yeah. Not sure who she is, but she called me up until I got here today. She was here yesterday, but there were so many people I couldn't point her out in the crowd. The one thing I know for sure is it's neither of you. At the time that I was getting the texts, you were both busy with the grand opening."

It got quiet for a second as we all sat and took everything in. I didn't know how this information would help them, or me for that matter, but it damn sure felt much better getting it out. I couldn't tell this information to the crew and be this transparent. It was hard always having to be tough all the time.

"I was getting texts from Chase's phone for a while too," the twin admitted. I could tell by the way the other girl turned around that she didn't know. "I was too scared to say anything, Skye. I didn't know what to do."

"Can I see the texts?" the one she called Skye asked. I made a mental note of her name and would get the twin's name before I left. I gave her the phone without hesitation, and they took a few seconds to read the texts. One just happened to come in at the time they were reading. They didn't really look like they knew who it was. They read them and gave the phone back without a word.

"I have no clue who that is, but it appears to be the same person who was texting me for a while. I never got a text from this new number, but I'd double down on it that it's the same person."

"I agree," I said, taking a breather for the first time in a while. "I have a private investigator on it, so as soon as I know something, I'll let you know," I lied. I didn't know these chicks from a can of paint. I just needed to know if they were who I thought they were, and from what I could see, they were hurt by the loss as well. This shit just didn't make any sense, but it would soon. I could feel it. For now, I could take the heat off of them.

"I'm sorry about what happened to your friend," Skye offered.

"Thank you. I appreciate that," I said awkwardly. "So I did actually come here to discuss business, but after all this, it may not be the time, Skye and . . ." I waited, leaving room for the other one to share her name.

"Selah," she responded, wiping a stray tear from her face. I remembered the campaign for her sister that she had once her body was found. I'd just have to go back and confirm the name.

"Maybe I can have you ladies come out to Miami so that we can discuss business soon. You ladies are on to something, and I'd love to be a part of it. My family is here, so I am in Philly often. I'm open to whatever I need to do to make this pop."

"That's perfect. I'll definitely be in touch," Skye responded as she came from around the desk, hand on her belly. Seeing her just made me miss my girl even more, and I couldn't wait to get back home. I decided that my time was up here, and I'd be flying out early if I could get a flight. As much as I loved Philly, it didn't love me back. The City of Brotherly Love wasn't set up that way.

When I got back out front, I made my way out before the fans could recognize me, and I dipped back to my grandma's house. I needed her to love up on me a little more before I left. I missed her so much, and I wanted to take her with me, but I understood that she was needed here. As my time came to an end and I got to the airport, I got another text from the number that I was avoiding. After reading it all, I gave her a simple text back and shut my phone off. I would be back, but it would be for her funeral.

Chapter 23

Vice

Losing My Grip

You're a dead bitch when I catch you.

Wow. Homeboy really just dismissed the fuck out of me. I thought for sure I had him in the bag, but somehow this shit flipped on me, and I wasn't sure how. I didn't even get a chance to snitch out Selah and secure the bag like I planned, but it's cool. I thought for now it was best to just let him be for a moment and put my focus back on my friends. These hoes had been hanging real tight lately. I was irritated that Skye didn't even ask me to help with the store, yet Selah's ass was right in the damn mix. I'd been saying it—they moved on without me, and it was fucked up.

How did I get my friends back without seeming like a snake? It wasn't like Selah was aware that

I tried to set her funky ass up. Skye was busy, too. Wait, was I tripping? These hoes owed me an apology! Here I was feeling bad thinking I did something wrong, when in reality they x'd me out of the equation. I didn't do a damn thing to them but ask for what was rightfully mine, and I shouldn't have had to ask for it since we were talking about it. It should have gone without saying, and I was hurt.

You know what they say. Hurt people hurt people. If I did nothing else before I moved out of Philly, I was going to make them wish they never tried to play me. Yeah, this could have easily been a conversation among sister-friends, but clearly my ass was delusional to even think that they had my back. *It's cool.* Sometimes the person you least expect is the one you have to lean on.

Bitch, stop past my crib. I need your help.

Before I could even get my safe good and closed, Renee was at my door ringing the bell. Pushing it closed, I made sure it was locked before I went to let her in. I decided not to keep my money in the bank just in case I needed to make a quick getaway. It was easier for me to travel with a duffle bag full of money than to try to get some shit from the bank. The way I was about to move, I couldn't be caught on camera.

"Hey, bitch, what was so urgent?" Renee asked as she made herself comfortable on my new sofa.

I didn't know how I was going to get out of the hood without my shit. I loved this couch, and I wanted my stuff, but I didn't necessarily want a damn U-Haul pulling up to the door. I didn't wany anyone to know I had money.

"How are things going at the boutique?" I asked as I poured us glasses of wine. I knew how she got down, and I offered her a little blue pill to go with her drink.

"I absolutely love it! Why didn't you tell me Skye was so dope, bitch? I wasn't even going in there on no management type shit, but the way this fashion sense is set up, honey . . ." she gushed, giving herself props.

I must say, Renee definitely could dress her ass off. She boosted the best shit from the malls and knew how to put a piece together out of rags. She was exactly who I needed on my team to get their asses back.

"Dope, huh?" I laughed as I took a long pull of my freshly rolled blunt. How was I going to paint these bitches in a light that would make her flip the script? She didn't know Selah or Skye the way I did. It shouldn't be too hard, but it looked like Skye already won her over.

"Yes! My commission check fitna be lit! I been eyeballing this bag at Neiman for a minute. Looks like I'm about to get that jawn," she said, leaning up into a slow twerk.

I swear, bitches who wasn't used to having shit were always impressed by bullshit like bags and shoes. It was me. I was bitches, and I felt exactly where she was coming from on that one.

"I feel you. I mean, not too bad for the store to only be open for a few days," I tossed out, trying not to sound salty. At one point I really wanted my friends to win, but it seemed lately they didn't want the same for me. One thing about Renee was she was about her paper. A guttersnipe, just like me. We'd do the right thing until we couldn't.

"I feel she's going to do really well. Philly needed another big-girl store. Ashley Stewart done went downhill."

"Yeah, I guess."

"Why haven't we seen you at anything? I thought y'all were tight."

"Yeah, me too. I wasn't invited," I lied to gauge her reaction. She was so damn gullible.

"Lies. I sent the texts out from Skye's phone, and I made sure your name was the first name I selected," she explained.

Shit. I would need to take a different approach with her. This bitch was Team Skye, and right now she couldn't do any wrong in her eyes. "My new phone or my old phone?"

"The phone you texted me from to get me here tonight, bitch."

Damn! She was on point tonight. It was cool. I was persistent.

"What's really up with y'all? Y'all used to be tighter than African braids. Now y'all acting all weird around each other."

How much do I tell this bitch? It's against the rules to spill tea on your squad, especially when you're in a space where you're not cool. You always end up regretting that shit later. I also knew who the hell I was talking to. Renee couldn't hold a tampon in her pussy, let alone some gossip. Anything I told her would definitely be all over the neighborhood by the morning.

"Money changes people," I tossed out into the atmosphere.

"Okay, as it should. The fuck! Let me get ahold of some good money, and I'm definitely acting different."

"So what if I said I had a way for you to come up on a nice piece of change?"

The look she gave me was half what the fuck was I talking about, and half what did she have to do. Money always talked, especially to hood rats, so I knew I was now talking her language.

"Okay, so here's the thing. . . ." I gave her this entire lic about how Skye scammed me out of money to open her store. I told her I was supposed to be partner, but when it came time to be active in the company, Skye chose Selah over me. She was becoming heated by the second as I spun a little truth in the mix. They definitely fell back from me after Sajdah's death. Neither of them reached out to see if I was okay or affected somehow by the shit we did, but I left most of those details out. Renee is one smart cookie.

She would definitely put one and three together if she had long enough to think about it.

"So basically, she owes me, but she's acting stupid like she don't know what it is."

"Wow. That's some foul shit. I'm shocked. She definitely doesn't seem like the type."

"Do they ever?"

"Truth."

We sat in silence for a little more while I watched the wheels spin in her head. I could see she was torn, because she probably felt like she was getting a good thing working at the store. Knowing how Skye operated, she probably was. Skye definitely looked out for those who looked out for her. She wanted her store to be successful, and who knew how much money Selah's nut ass invested in the company? I hated both of them bitches, and I wanted them to feel my pain.

"What do I need to do?"

"So there's this guy," I began as I kind of put her on to Goon and how we needed to get the bag from him too. Both Selah and Skye were going to regret leaving me out. I wasn't above putting both they asses in the ground right on top of each other. Renee wasn't the type of ride-or-die bitch like I was with my crew, but with some grooming, I could get her where I needed her to be.

"Okay, cool. Let me see how things move in this store for a few more weeks, and then we'll come up with a plan. You know she's due soon, and I'm pretty sure I'll have control of the store while she's out."

"Indeed," I responded as we continued to smoke and drink. I eventually ordered some food, and when I went to get the money out of the safe, she was coming out of the bathroom and peeped the scene. I felt like I closed the door before she could really look, but she definitely saw something. I could tell because her demeanor changed a little once the food came, and she kept asking me questions about how much money she would get. Hopefully I wouldn't have to body her ass too. We'd just have to wait and see how this thing went. One thing I learned was patience when it came to dealing with Skye and Selah. Line all them ducks up first, then pluck they ass off one at a time. By the time she left, I had her all the way on board. I just had to come up with a plan where I could strike and get the fuck out of dodge before I was caught up.

Chapter 24

Selah

Strike First

"Bitch, do you think he knows what we did?"

The way this paranoia is set up, it took everything in me not to fall at this man's feet and beg for his forgiveness for killing his friend. When we read those texts, they had Vice written all over them. I didn't need to see a name. Once a scammer, always a scammer. This chick was really out to get us. She was definitely the type to throw your ass under the bus, then check to make sure you were under there good. That shit hurt more than her being caught on tape at my man's house. On more than one occasion, might I add. I didn't blame her completely for fucking Chase. From what I saw on the tape, he didn't put up any fight. He probably thought he was keeping her quiet. She probably thought she was doing me a favor. At this time and place, fuck them both.

Sigh. This shit was too much to deal with. I wanted
to go down to her house and squeeze her neck until
her head popped off, but I knew I couldn't handle
Vice like that. When I got her, it would have to be a
permanent situation. You can't give people like Vice
a chance to strike back. My sister deserved a second
chance. Hell, even Chase deserved some redemption.
Vice? She deserved everything she had coming.

"Naw. He wouldn't have been able to sit through
that knowing we were the people who killed his
people. He would have gotten rid of us on the spot.
As far as Vice . . . you already know what we gotta do,"
Skye responded as she sipped her water.

I could tell from the way her face was twisting up
that the baby was kicking and making her uncomfortable. She was probably having an episode of Braxton
Hicks. I didn't think she was going to make it to her
due date with all that was going on.

"Agreed. He was fishing for information. I do feel
like he thought we might know the person," I responded, my mind racing a mile a minute. I wondered briefly what my payback would be for this.
Surely it would be something heinous.

"We do. Vice did it."

"I pulled the trigger."

"Because that bitch set you up. Hear me out," she
began as she shifted in her seat to get comfortable.
"I've been thinking about this for a while, and I didn't
really want to place blame, but here it is. She came

to me with the picture of them early on. I'll admit at first I was looking at Sajdah crazy, but it just didn't sit right. That's why I told her we needed more evidence before we came to you. Shit don't always look the way we see it, sis. You know how you are. We need concrete evidence when dealing with you. You see what happened to Kevin."

Silence. She had me pegged, and I couldn't deny it. It's the "shoot you in the head without hesitation" for me. My temper was so out of control these days, and I thanked God for my therapist daily. It was crazy that I wasn't sitting in somebody's jail cell or a padded cell in a crazy house. They knew me, and I appreciated them for it.

"Now I do feel like she had good intentions in the beginning. She didn't want you hurt. She didn't want to be the one who hurt you. That's when shit got fuzzy. She may or may not have had some personal shit with Sajdah from when we were kids. You know they never got along. Did she have to fuck your man to prove her point? No, but that's what guttersnipes do. She's not cut from the same cloth as us, Selah. We've said that since we were young. You can take the girl out of the ghetto, but you can't take the ghetto out of the girl. Hell, we can't even take the girl out of the ghetto. Her ass refuses to leave."

"But I killed my sister." I began to cry.

"Because she set you up. You know damn well you wouldn't have responded like that under normal circumstances. Your sister told you the truth, and you just weren't ready for it. Do I wish things turned out differently? Absolutely. I miss the hell out of Sajdah. You were emotional, and shit happened that was out of your control. Now we get her ass back. Period."

Boom! And there it is. I'm not going to say I whole-heartedly agreed with Skye. Let's just be honest for a second. I didn't have to kill my sister. Was I set up? I never thought about it that way. She definitely played in my face, and that was something I had to deal with. I said I wasn't going to kill anyone else, but I thought I could make an exception for Vice. She was out to get me first, that was for sure. So I had to move first if I was going to survive the fight. We had to be strategic with this one, although this one might be a little bit easier. Vice didn't have anyone who cared enough about her to hunt her down if she went missing, so we didn't have to worry about that. This had to be a clean mission though. I would not be able to live with myself if something happened to Skye or her baby.

"You're right. Let's talk away from this setting. Right now we move like everything is Gucci."

We wrapped up our conversation and went back out front to handle things in the store. I'm not going to lie. This shit had my stomach in knots. I hated that potentially I had to kill someone I used to care about. Lies to the side, I still cared about her. It was just harder when you knew the truth about someone. It caught me off guard when she popped up in that footage. The audio wasn't the best, but the picture was crystal fucking clear. From the way she looked around when she got out of the car, she definitely followed him there the first time. They had some kind of altercation at the door, and then next thing I knew, he was balls deep in this bitch. I had to run to the bathroom and throw up. That shit had my stomach twisted like you wouldn't believe. I fast-forwarded through the rest, and she was there more times than I cared to see. Random girls I could accept. That's the stupid shit drug dealers do. Friends and family hit at the gut, and I couldn't handle it. What fucked me up more was the day that they came to meet me for lunch, she asked for his address like she didn't know where he lived. *I gotta give it to her. At least she kept up the charade until the very end.*

I knew how to get her though. Money always moved Vice. That would be her downfall. I just had to find a way to get her where I needed her to be. We would have to wait a little because Skye was carrying my niece or nephew at the moment, and I needed her. I didn't trust this type of heist with anyone else. I could go kill her by myself for sure, but I'd need help moving the body. I didn't want to make any hasty decisions, so we would just bide our time.

When I got back home, I found my mom sitting in the middle of the living room floor with pictures spread out all around her. Most of the photos were of Sajdah and me together, but I could clearly see as

I got closer that she had picked out the pictures with Sajdah alone. I wondered if her therapist told her to do this. As I got closer, further inspection showed that the pictures with us together were cut in half, and some of the ones of me were ripped into pieces. *Wow!* Did she hate me for real?

"Mom, what's happening here?" I asked as I got up on her. I looked around briefly for my dad and quickly concluded that he was probably taking a much-needed nap while this loony tune was out here acting crazy.

"Well, my therapist told me that I needed to come to some sort of closure," she answered with a slight laugh behind it. It was like she couldn't even believe it was even suggested. "Everybody always wants you to make adjustments because it makes them uncomfortable. The thing is, I don't give a flying rat's ass how uncomfortable anybody feels around me. Nobody is going to tell me I have to forget it, get past it, move on from it, or any combination of the above. I will do so in my time. I miss my baby," she ended, breaking down in tears.

I immediately rushed over to her side to comfort her. She was right. Who was I to judge her for feeling how she felt, especially when I put her in that dark space? I ended up on the floor with her, holding her like a baby as she released her tears and frustration into my chest. I wished I could take this pain from her, and I wondered if me leaving would make her feel better. I was a constant reminder of what she no longer had. Just maybe if I moved on, she could too. My dad would disagree, but he would understand. It was time for me to go. That was the only thing I felt would save her from herself.

When she was able to gather herself, I helped her up from the floor and up the steps to her bedroom. Just as I thought, my dad was inside sleeping, and he sat up when I opened the door. The look on his face told me that he knew she must have had an episode, and he immediately got up to get her in the bed properly.

"Let's chat once she's settled," I said to him as he climbed in bed behind my mother to hold her some more. I worried about my dad. He was really what was keeping me here. He didn't say much, not since the funeral. He was always at our beck and call, and I had to know how he was holding up. It was almost like he couldn't break down because my mother and I were always in some state of distress. It wasn't fair to him, and he needed an escape too.

A few hours passed before my dad found me in the kitchen eating ice cream directly from the container. Here I was again eating my sorrows. He grabbed a spoon and took the seat next to me, digging into the container and taking a heaping spoonful of our favorite dessert. I loved my dad so much. It killed me that I put him in this position. We sat in silence for a while before I broke the silence. I couldn't take the sound of quiet in this house anymore.

"Dad, can I be honest with you, and you not hate me?" I asked on the verge of tears. I felt like if I just told one person, no matter the consequences, at least I got to tell my story.

"I could never hate you, baby," he replied as he set his spoon down and gave me his full attention. I hesitated because I didn't want the only man I ever loved to feel differently about me. I wouldn't be able to handle it if he no longer loved me.

"It's my fault Sajdah is gone."

Silence.

He looked at me, and I looked at him, scared to say any more. He reached over and took my hand, and for the first time I saw a tear run down his face. I almost lost it, but I knew now wasn't the time. This wasn't about me. This was about him being allowed to release his emotions.

"I believe you," he said, shocking me into silence even further. "And I don't want you to ever repeat it again. I don't need the details. I just need you to know I forgive you for whatever it is you've done, and your mother will forgive you in time. Never speak of this again. Just promise me that," he pleaded as tear after tear fell from his chin and hit the table.

"I'm sorry, Daddy."

"I know you are, baby. We've all done a thing or two that we are not proud of. Those are the things you take to the grave."

The way he came and hugged me, gosh, you have no idea how this made me feel. I held on to him just as tight as I prepared myself mentally to leave. I didn't want to go, but I knew I had to. I had to give them room and time to grieve. This was for the best. As I leaned back, I looked into my dad's eyes, and I saw the pain there. Would he have said anything to me ever? At this point it didn't even matter. I was just happy that he understood what I needed to do.

"I'll be out in a few weeks. I'll contact a Realtor in the morning."

He held me again and kissed my forehead before leaving to go be with my mom. All of a sudden, I felt claustrophobic. I ran upstairs to my room and locked myself inside. I couldn't believe I was even entertaining the thought of leaving this house. I was planning to be here forever. I sat on the side of the bed and took in the four walls that surrounded me. I grew up in here. I protected my sissy from the boogeyman in here. I cried over a guy or ten in here. Maybe, just maybe, it was time for me to go.

I got up to take a quick shower, and I could hear my mom and dad conversing in their room. I crept over so that I could hear better, and I felt like I was violating their privacy, yet I couldn't turn away.

"We have to let her go. It's time," my dad explained to my mom.

"So she just gets to leave us here to pick up the pieces? I told you Sajdah came to me and told me everything."

"Listen, enough of that talk. She needs our support now. She's hurt too," my dad jumped in. They were in there arguing over me. That shit just brought me down even lower.

"Not sure why. You can't be the villain and the victim at the same time."

I turned and went back to my room, opting to skip the shower. Instead, I started packing my things. I would find a storage facility in the morning and stay in a hotel until a house came through. *I may just grab an apartment in the burbs or something.* I just knew I wasn't staying here longer than I had to.

I heard my phone buzz on the bed, and I started to ignore it because I didn't feel like any more bad news. Picking it up anyway, I looked to see who it was. No one was left who truly cared about me, so I was unsure of who it could be. I put two and two together and came to the conclusion that Vice had Chase's phone, so those texts no longer scared me.

We need to talk tonight, Skye texted me. I sent her a thumbs-up emoji, then lay down and made myself as comfortable as I could in my bed. This shit hurt more than I wanted to admit. I just held on to the hope that one day we would all be in a better place, be it on the dirt or in it.

Chapter 25

Skye

Listen Actively, Then Act on It

"Can I talk to you for a second?"

Renee and I were alone in the store, and I felt that she wanted to talk. It had been a few weeks since my meeting with Selah and Charles, who we found out was Chase's close friend Goon. I had to go do some research and ask a few people I could trust down the way who he was. Apparently, he was big in Philly, breaking ankles on the court for years before his church family paid for him to go to college in addition to the scholarship he had received. He later ended up being drafted by Miami Heat, and after coming back to the hood to get his longtime girlfriend, he'd been in Miami ever since. I wasn't all the way sure how he met Chase, aside from them being in college together, and I got that information from Selah. They used to sell drugs at one point while in college. Chase somehow migrated to Philly, and Goon migrated to the NBA.

This shit sitting on my chest was so heavy I could barely breathe. Did I want to get rid of another friend? Not necessarily, but it wasn't looking like I had much of a choice. I tried weighing the pros and cons of letting her live, but it wasn't looking good for her at the moment. We had to do something. She couldn't be trusted. I also began to think how long it would be, or if it would ever get to the point where I'd have to make this same decision regarding Selah. We'd been in this thing forever. Why did it have to end up this way?

My heart was heavy, and my stomach was heavy from this baby getting increasingly more difficult to hold in. It was like the baby was getting antsy from my anxiety and wanted out. He still had a little more time to bake, so I just had to be patient. I really didn't want to hear shit Renee had to say. I was just trying to stay in one piece and couldn't handle any more bad news. Was she about to quit on me? She was the best employee ever, and she got the other girls in line as well. I couldn't take a loss right now, and hopefully I was just overreacting. Getting up, I wobbled to the back while the rest of the fashionistas helped shoppers with their items.

"What's going on, Renee?" I tried to sound upbeat as I made my way to my desk on feet swollen three times their normal size. I set my phone to record, and set it facedown under the desk out of view. My anxiety had me feeling like my throat was closing, and I had to take a few deep breaths to fight back the urgency. I just hoped she assumed I was uncomfortable due to the pregnancy and not her presence.

"So I have a question and possibly some information for you. But the way the hood is set up, you didn't get this information from me."

"Okay," I said, sounding puzzled. Where was she going with this? I braced myself for the worst because I knew it was coming.

"I'm just going to say it," she said, taking a seat in front of me. "How cool are you and Vice?"

"That's my girl! I love her. Why do you ask?" Now she had my damn attention. This girl was really starting to work my set, and I was so disappointed in Vice. If knowing someone forever and not knowing them at all were a person, Vice would be that person. This shit was making me feel sick the more I learned about her.

"Well, just because you've known someone a long time doesn't make them your friend. That's just someone you've known for a long time."

"Okay," I said, sitting back in my seat, my child's foot feeling like it was lodged in my rib cage. "I'm not good with riddles, and this is not a game show. Either you're going to say what you need to say, or we are done with this conversation."

I could tell that she was battling with wanting to say whatever it was she had to say or just holding on to it. She had to know that it could possibly jeopardize her employment. I didn't know how important it was to her, but I was about to find out.

"I don't want people I can't trust in my organization," I said to her with a straight face, tossing the ball back into her court. She had better decide wisely. That was all I had to say about that. She got up, and I thought she was about to leave, but she actually locked the door. This had to be some serious shit if she was concerned about someone walking in on us. I was starting to get nervous, but I held it together.

"Vice is not your friend."

"How do you know?"

"Because she asked me to set you up to get robbed."

"Really?" *Wow, Vice. Is this what we've come to?* I didn't want to believe it, but why would she lie?

"Really."

I struggled to keep my mouth from falling open. "I need more details than that."

"She called me to her house a few weeks ago, not long after the grand opening. She tried to say that she wasn't invited and that's why she didn't show up, but I stopped that lie right in its tracks. I sent the texts out personally myself. She was telling me about some guy she was trying to extort for money, but that you and the twin you're always with played in her face regarding some money y'all were supposed to split equally but didn't. It looked like she had a bunch of money already, because when I came from using the restroom, she was getting money out of a safe, and that bitch was stuffed to the max with money. Excuse my language," she said, dropping her eyes briefly.

"That's weird because she did actually show up. It's no problem though. We're both grown. Continue," I urged as I made sure my phone was still recording. I wasn't sure why I even thought about recording the conversation before coming in here, but I was glad that I was proactive in that respect. I needed Selah to hear this for herself.

"At any rate, she asked if I liked working here, and she offered me a nice lump sum to help her rob you. She didn't say exactly when. I told her the store was new, so I didn't know what the activity would be like months from now. I know you're due to go out in about four weeks, and I didn't want some shit to happen while you were gone and you be looking at me funny. We've only been here a few weeks, but you've been good to me. Vice is just somebody I know from down the way. We're not friends like that. After seeing how she would do someone who is really a friend, I don't know that I even want to be involved with her at all. I didn't commit to anything, I just wanted to bring it to your attention so that you knew how to move properly."

Silence. The kind that was so loud it felt like everyone in the world could hear it. "How much did she offer you?"

"A hundred thousand," she answered. She didn't blink, and her eye contact remained steady.

"And tell me again why you are telling me this? What's in it for you?"

"It's the loyalty for me," she began confidently. "I believe in karma. You hired me and you pay me well. Shit, with the way these commissions been looking, I can make a hundred thousand myself. You are good to us. You deserved to know who's in your camp. I know how cool you all are. I was never in the circle, but we all see how y'all get down. What she doing ain't cool."

I took it all in. It was hurtful, but I could dig it. However, I wasn't sure how much I could trust Renee. Why would she just bring me this information if she didn't want anything out of it? Yeah, she could probably make her own money, but a hundred racks up front had to be hard to turn down. Something wasn't sitting right with me, and my Spidey-Sense was starting to tingle. Would we be digging a grave in the hood for her too? I wanted to call Selah up right now, but I had to move smarter than this.

"Okay, here's what you're going to do. We never had this conversation, okay? You keep moving like you been moving with Vice. I don't need an informant, so you don't have to keep bringing information back to me. I'll handle her accordingly. If she decides she wants to rob my boutique, let her. I'll handle her the way I need to handle her. I do appreciate the

information, and I'll have something for you soon.
There's no need to be paranoid. Do not discuss this
with the other fashionistas. Do not let Vice know we
had this conversation. Understood?"

"Completely."

She got up and left, and I locked the door behind
her so that no one would walk in on me. She was being reckless, and I was over it. I sent Selah a message
letting her know to stop past my house later tonight.
I couldn't wait to tell her this shit. Just to play devil's
advocate, I picked up my phone and pulled up Vice's
name in my contacts. I started to call her, but I was
too heated to disguise my disgust with her and opted
to send a text instead. Since she wanted to be on
some fake shit, I decided to give her a little rope.

Hey, bestie! When are you coming back to see my
store?

The message went from delivered to read quickly.
I wondered if she thought something was awkward
about me texting her, but I quickly dismissed it. After
all, we were going through something minor right
now, but as far as she was concerned, she was still a
friend of mine.

Hey, boo! You were super busy at the grand opening, so we didn't get a chance to chat, but let's do
lunch tomorrow? I'll stop by the boutique tomorrow
and bring lunch from Chickie's & Pete's.

See, she thought I was slow. She wanted to see
what the back of the store looked like so that she

knew how to set me up. Little did she know I was ready to show her because that would be the last setup she'd ever do. People like Vice you had to stay ten steps ahead of. I appreciated Renee for giving me the information, but now her ass was on the radar too. *You don't drop gems like that and don't expect nothing in return. She gotta be quicker than that.* I'd see what she wanted in due time. There was no way she was convincing me that she did it because she loved her job that much. *Try again, sis.*

Later that night as we were closing the store, my favorite security guard came by to help me with the gate, and we chatted as he made sure I made it to the train station safely. I was so occupied with what I learned today that I clearly ignored him flirting with me. I made the drop at the bank and hopped on the train to get to my car. This baby was really kicking the hell out of me, and it took my breath a few times.

I texted Selah to let her know I was on my way home so that she could make her way over. It wasn't long before she got there, and thankfully the baby settled down. She had a bag of food from Olive Garden, and I was happy because I was hungry.

"What's going on, sis?" she asked as she unbagged the food and got us plates from the kitchen. Instead of responding, I just took my phone out and played the audio from Renee. I watched my friend go from confused to shocked to disbelieving just like I did earlier in the day. Pretty soon, the anger showed up as well.

"That slimy bitch!" she yelled as she jumped up and began pacing back and forth. "I been saying that about her. Ever since the incident with Sajdah, she been on some other shit. I'm about to go get her ass now!"

She went to grab her car keys, but I was able to stop her. "You don't have to do that. I have a plan."

"What's the plan? Because I'm ready to hurt her ass today."

"She's bringing me lunch tomorrow to the boutique."

"You're letting her come to the store?" she screamed in disbelief.

"Yep, so that she can see what she needs to see for the setup. You know Vice. She's going to plot and plan this shit out. She'll think that the door in the back leads to the outside, when in reality it's just a trash area that the mall cleans once a week. Our door doesn't have an outside entrance, and there's a camera on both sides. I want her to think that I'm slow to what she's doing. I know her. She's going to wait until I go out on leave to put her plan into action. She thinks she has Renee in her pocket. The minute she makes a move, we go get her ass."

"So you're telling me I have to wait to pop this bitch in the face?"

"I'm telling you to come have lunch with us tomorrow. It could be fun."

The smile that spread across her face scared the shit out of me. She had that same look when we went to check Chase, and we ended up with a body in the trunk. She could not shoot this girl in my damn store! I had too much to lose. My baby was at stake at this point, and I could not jeopardize his life fucking around with Vice.

"Selah, just come have lunch. Things will work out the way they are supposed to. Leave the gun at home."

She agreed to come after contemplating it for a second or so more. I'd have to keep my eye on her ass tomorrow. Vice had a way of pushing your buttons when she knew that she had you, and I was not in the position to break up a fight with these hoes. As we finally broke bread, I urged Selah to just trust me on this one.

"Friend, things will work out exactly how they're supposed to. You have to trust me on this."

"I trust you. I just don't trust myself."

Chapter 26

Vice

Scoping the Scene

Sitting on a million or more felt different. For once I wasn't feeling like I had to worry about shit. For the first time in my adult life, I was able to go into the market and buy food without using food stamps or having to put something back because I didn't have enough. I didn't have to fake pregnant and stuff meats in my hoodie pockets or go through self-checkout and only pay for half my shit. This bitch was rich, ya hear me? And it felt damn good, no cap.

It also felt out of place. Like I needed to move on. I slipped up and let Renee see inside the safe. I'd been paranoid ever since. All I needed was the hood to find out that I had a little bit of money, and automatically a price would be on my head. All loyalty, too, would go out the window, and every nigga I fucked or sucked would be gunning for me. I had to go sooner rather than later, and I knew it. I spent most mornings looking at apartments in the country. It was far enough away from the hood but close enough to get back quickly. I didn't want just anything though. I had a few dollars and felt like I wanted to splurge a little.

The dumb shit was my credit was ass. There weren't many places checking for me, even when I offered to pay the first year's rent up front. I had one more place that I was hoping would look past the small credit issue and let me in. Selah and Skye had been telling me to get my credit in order for years, and now I truly understood what they meant. No credit is worse than bad credit. I didn't go to college, so I didn't have student loans. I didn't have any credit cards. Nothing. Folks didn't know if they could trust me, but that wasn't a first. It'd been like this all my life.

I ordered food for Skye and me while I was out so that by the time I got down to the District, I could just pick it up and go. I didn't really get a chance to look at the boutique when I was there, so I was interested to see what she had done with the place. Renee was hype as shit that Skye basically let her do what she wanted with the place, and I must say I was very impressed when I got there. When I walked in the door, the ladies they called fashionistas all greeted me with a smile, and I immediately was teamed up with a personal stylist to help me pick out some looks.

"I'm just here for lunch. Is Skye in?" I asked the young lady who was trying to help me. At that moment I saw her wobbling from the back, Renee at her side carrying several shoeboxes for her client. She gave me a smile and kept right on to the front of the store to help the woman pair some shoes with the look she was currently wearing. This shit was on point, and I was so mad I wasn't a part of it. This wasn't just some shopping. This experience was an entire vibe. None of this shit was cheap either, judging by the few price tags I peeped as we made our way to the back.

These ladies were prepared to have you snatched and ready to go by the time you left up out of here, so once you got to the register and saw that tab, you felt better about paying it. From the shapewear to the finishing touches of jewelry, they had you covered. I wasn't mad about any of it. This was the kind of attention you got in high-end boutiques and stores like Gucci and Fendi. They treated you like a queen as they lavished you in the best. That was the way it was supposed to be, and I was glad to see that my friend modeled her store in the same fashion.

"Hey, love, glad you could make it," Skye said, giving me a hug the best way she could considering how big her belly had gotten.

It seemed to grow by the day. She looked like she was ready to pop at any moment. Better her than my ass. I was not about to let a child ruin the tight grip on my pussy. I guessed I'd be living motherhood vicariously through her ass. As long as there was a clinic equipped with a table and a vacuum, I'd always be kid free.

When we got to the back, I was blown away by her office space. The colors, the layout, the furniture, everything looked absolutely amazing. I set the food down and took the liberty of running my hands through the racks of clothing she had off to the side, taking note of the security door that probably led to somewhere on the side of the building. I took note of the numbers 1212A that were displayed on the door and made a mental note to see where on the outside of the building was the other side. Or maybe it didn't lead outside at all. I tried to think if I ever noticed any side doors when it was the Gallery. This was a brand-new building, so the floor plan might be different.

She sat patiently while I combed through the shoeboxes that displayed my size and began putting some looks to the side. I planned to pay for whatever I had, but I did wonder if she would just let me slide with the items. After all, we were besties, right?

"You should let one of my fashionistas style you and get the entire experience."

"Maybe I will," I replied as I backed away from the jewelry. She had some really nice stuff here. The least I could do was support my friend by making a purchase. I planned to get that back and more sooner than she thought. "For now let's eat."

We sat and began dishing out the food. I couldn't believe how hungry I was all of a sudden. When I got nervous I got like that sometimes. As I looked at her, I almost felt bad about what I was going to do to her. Like a tiny bit bad, but not enough to not do it, you dig? We ate in silence as I took in my surroundings. She really made something for herself. This made me wonder how much money she got from Selah. I didn't know how much it cost to open a boutique, but this shit was hot like fish grease. Everything about it screamed money. Did she dump all she had into this? Were she and Selah partners? Why didn't they include me? Just when I was going to ask, I heard the office door open, and I made eye contact with Selah. It took everything in me not to swing on her ass.

"Hey, bitches," she yelled as she pranced in, first hugging me then hugging Skye. Who was this new bitch? I was expecting old, depressed, red-eyed, "ain't slept in ten months" Selah. This ho looked refreshed as fuck, and that shit caught me way off guard.

"Hey, love! Pull up a seat and get a plate. What brought you here today?" Skye asked as Selah made herself comfortable, helping herself to the food I bought for me and Skye.

My face was turning more sour by the minute, and it was a struggle holding it together. I wasn't here for her, but maybe it was a blessing that she showed up. I'd had some shit I'd been dying to say to her for a while. Maybe now was the time.

"I was at Burlington with my mom, chile," she said, rolling her eyes in her head as if she was annoyed. "She wanted to come by and see the boutique. Your fashionistas are out there styling her now."

"Yaassss, Mrs. Tracy! She better get that experience!" Skye responded as the two laughed lovingly. I, on the other hand, was feeling like a pressure cooker ready to explode.

"Hey, friend, long time no see, or hear, or anything since I saw you at the bank. What's been going on with you?" Selah inquired, both girls now with their attention on me.

"Oh, you know." I hesitated as I swallowed what was in my mouth. "Just trying to figure out how to live since, you know . . ."

"I understand. The bounce back has been difficult," Selah responded.

Her disposition was off. She was friendly as fuck for some reason, but her eyes were throwing unavoidable daggers. "About the last time I saw you, sorry I was acting weird. There was a lot going on that day."

"No need to apologize. It's like that sometimes."

"Yeah, it is."

We all chewed in silence for a while, lost in thought. I couldn't believe it'd gotten to the point where I was really contemplating robbing my friend's boutique and shooting the other one right in the temple. There was a definite disconnect, but was it mendable? Did I

want it? After quick contemplation I came to the conclusion that I didn't. My mom always told me to be a
loner. She'd never steered me wrong. *Fuck both these
bitches.* She always told me to keep my enemies close.
We were conjoined triplets out of this bitch as far as
I was concerned. And to think I put my pussy on the
line for these hoes. I needed to learn how to mind my
damn business. Seriously.

"How do we get back how we used to be?" Skye
questioned, wincing and grabbing her belly afterward.

That baby was tearing her ass up. I laughed on the
inside low-key.

"I don't know that we can," I responded and stuffed
a shrimp in my mouth. "The trust is gone." The look I
got from Selah, man, if looks could kill, I'd have been
stretched out in a casket at this very moment.

"I mean, it doesn't have to be. We've all done some
shit. At a time like this we need to pull together
instead of drifting apart. We need each other. At least
I do. Y'all know y'all all I got."

Was this ho about to cry? I was not beat for this
emotional pregnant shit. Would Selah really want to
be my friend if she knew all the details? I had been
setting Chase's dumb ass up for months for her. She
wouldn't see it that way, though. They never do.

"I feel like it's something that can be worked on," I
replied nonchalantly. I needed her to be comfortable.
She was about to get got, and I didn't want her to
think I had anything to do with it.

"I agree," Selah responded as she got up to put her plate in the garbage.

You ever just want to drag somebody on the spot? I wanted her ass bad, but today I'd let her live.

"Let me go see what kind of damage my mom done caused out here. I'm sure she has one of everything on her tab by now."

"Yes, let's go see. I'm glad to see her trying to get back to some kind of normalcy," Skye replied.

"I mean, we're working on it. That's all we can do."

"Y'all go ahead. I'm going to clean this stuff up and bring my little pile out front."

"Okay, cool. Meet you out front."

As they exited, I put the unfinished food in a bag and gathered up the trash to go into the can. I wanted to open the door to see where it led, but I didn't know if it would sound an alarm of some sort. I started to just do it anyway, and just tell her I was looking for a dumpster, but decided against it. I did check and didn't see any obvious cameras, but I'd just ask Renee for more details. Gathering my things, I made my way out front just in time to catch Selah and her mom at the register.

"Vicerean, its good seeing you," she said as I approached them all. "I haven't seen you since you stopped by the house to use the bathroom that day. How have you been?"

"Oh, I've been good, Mrs. Tracy. Just staying off the radar." I didn't miss the look Selah gave me then her mom. Shit, her mom low-key just ratted me out. *Fuck it though*. If she didn't say shit, I wasn't saying shit.

"I can totally understand. Well, you ladies have a great rest of your day. I'm going home to give my husband a fashion show!"

We all laughed as they exited, and I got in line to ring my items up next. I didn't miss the look on Skye's face either. No doubt she was talking about the day I came and got the earring and bra pics in the bathroom. I went right to Skye afterward, so she knew exactly what she was talking about. Hopefully Selah just let it be what it was and didn't put too much thought into it. I was already on her ass as it was. It wouldn't be anything to change the plan and take her simple ass out first.

Once I swiped my card, I gave Skye another hug and thanked her for her time, although I couldn't help but feel like this was a little ambush. Selah could have very well just been stopping by, or it could have been planned. I didn't give a damn either way. I was still going to do what was best for me.

As I made my way to my truck, I tried calling Chase's friend once more, and the phone just rang. He didn't even bother to just send me to voicemail anymore. I wasn't sure how the dynamic changed, but I had one more trick up my sleeve for his ass, too. At this point I didn't give a damn who I threw under the bus. As long as they were out of my face and out of my way, we were good.

Chapter 27

Selah

It's Showtime!

Let's just take a step back for a minute. So when Skyc and Vice came to me the day I killed Chase, I was already having a moment with him. I need you to understand something about me. I came from a full house. I'd never lived with anyone besides my parents and my sister, so moving in with Chase was new to me. Foreign territory, if you will. Something I thought I was ready for but definitely was the fuck not. I learned that lesson the hard way. I didn't know what I thought it was going to be, but what I wanted and what I got weren't the same. Too bad we can't get a do-over.

Yes, I knew he was a drug dealer. That was kind of why I liked him so much. Yes, I knew it was a possibility that he would not be home a lot. But for real, when did this man sleep? Yes, I wanted it to change. Maybe I should have communicated that better.

"I don't know if that's a good idea, Selah. What if he tries to kill us?"

That entire experience was brand-spanking new to me, and I felt alone. My sister wasn't speaking to me, and Chase just wasn't giving me what I needed in a man. I felt like he was cheating on me. When I found the fucking earing and panties in the bathroom, it put another nail in the coffin, but I really tried to give this man some wiggle room. That shit might have been old. I never thought that there was a possibility that it belonged to my sister. I was emotional that day. My mom didn't offer me any solace, and I just needed something, anything to just be right. Make this shit make sense.

Was I expecting my best friends to come to me with evidence that would ultimately kill the love of my life? Nope. I didn't want to believe it. I wanted to walk into the house and ask him to explain himself. He would tell me a half-truth, and we would be back regular by the weekend. That was the plan.

Selah, why didn't you leave the gun in the safe?

I asked myself that question at least ten times a day every day, even now. They'd been dead and gone for almost a year at this point. Why was I even bothering trying to change the narrative now? I knew the answer. I pulled the fucking heater out because someone was going to catch that shit.

The sound left the universe before I got up the steps, so if my friends were trying to talk me out of it, I wouldn't have heard them anyway. It was like I was watching myself move in slow motion through the house as I made my way upstairs. I wanted to stop myself, but my body wasn't listening to me. The sounds coming from the bedroom were controlling my feet.

Did I expect to see my face when I opened the bedroom door? Nope. I was hoping it was a random chickenhead who we would beat the brakes off of and send on her merry way, jumping his ass afterward. Why the fuck did it have to be Sajdah? For that moment my heart stopped beating. My eyes could hardly register what I was seeing. One deep breath and the sound came back to the world, and I could see, hear, and smell everything. My arm rose, and you know the rest.

"He won't. He came looking for answers. We're going to let him know who is responsible for the death of his friend. Yeah, I killed him, but because of Vice. She set this entire thing up just like you said, right? He doesn't need to know every detail. We will take care of her. As far as he's concerned, she killed Chase and my sister. The end."

"Selah, I don't know about this," Skye insisted. She'd always been a Nervous Nancy. At moments like this, it was very annoying.

"Listen, you just take care of my handsome nephew. I'll handle the rest. Just be ready to rock when I say, 'Roll.' I love you, friend."

"I love you more."

Once the call was disconnected, I sat back and took a deep breath. It had been a few weeks since the incident at the boutique. It wasn't lost on me that my mom mentioned seeing Vice.

When my mom said it, it was like another piece of the puzzle clicked into place. She recalled the day vividly as if it had just happened. Vice stopped by to use the bathroom, and she made her a plate to go. She must have been desperate at that point to find anything she could to frame my sister. After the shooting, I sat one night looking at the photo evidence that Vice and Skye had presented. Out of all the photos, I wondered how they were able to get a pic of the bra and earring. I kept looking at the picture, trying to decipher why it looked so familiar to me. When I moved back home the week before killing Sajdah, I found myself in the bathroom thinking about the pics again. I saw the bra and the earring on the floor, but the shit didn't click at the moment. I was still grieving killing Chase, so I wasn't looking for any more evidence.

Vice. She'd always been a jealous, hating-ass whore. Sajdah had said it. I just never let it sink in. I picked the perfect time to want to listen. But life goes on, right? And one day we wake up and the pain is now a dull ache that we've learned to get used to. I felt like I could have happiness again . . . eventually.

Just as I imagined, Skye had her baby a week before her due date. She was so uncomfortable. I knew that baby was trying to make an escape. I was just glad it was one of those nights that I was staying the night at her house. I found myself an apartment in Yeadon, away from everything and everyone. It was quiet, too quiet actually, and sometimes I just needed company. No one knew I was here except for my dad. He almost didn't know either, but he insisted just in case something happened. I kept that information from Skye also. As far as she was concerned, I was still at home with my parents.

When I packed my room, this time I took every damn thing I owned. I didn't leave much of anything behind like I did when I went to stay with Chase. The only thing I left was the bed, and I stayed at Skye's house for a few days until my bedroom furniture was delivered. I decided I wouldn't get any other furniture until I got a house. The apartment was just temporary until I was done house hunting. I was working with an amazing Realtor who was helping me look for a good home. I didn't need a whole bunch of house. Just enough for me to grow in. Nafisa Bunch was the shit when it came to getting these homes in order, so I was patiently waiting my turn and letting her handle her business.

I also quit my job. No one knew that either. I did the right thing and turned in my two weeks' notice, just in case I got bored and wanted to come back. Cici was so sad about it. We had been office mates for almost six years. At first she tried to convince me to just go on leave, but in reality, they needed to give that position to someone who needed the money. I was good in that respect. I promised her that we'd hang out soon, and as I packed myself to leave, we got one last hug in before I dipped. It was definitely bittersweet.

For the first time in a while, it felt like I could breathe, and that felt amazing. I felt like I was getting great traction with my therapist, and I was really ready to start walking in my purpose. I just had to handle Vice first. I needed a clean slate, and I was taking this time to get everything out of the way before I completely moved on.

We were just waiting for her to strike. Skye went out on leave unexpectedly, so Renee had to jump in and handle the store operations while she was out. I came through a few days a week to help out and make sure the books were in order and everything was going well. Skye and I had a conversation with Renee about the entire Vice conversation, and after we promised her the contents of Vice's safe once we got rid of her, she was on board for whatever. I wasn't 100 percent sure that I could trust Renee, so we limited what we told her, but the most important thing for her to do was to keep shit going with Vice the way it'd been going. We would handle the rest.

I dialed Goon's number a few times but just couldn't get myself to press that TALK button. Honestly, I was nervous as shit. I didn't know who he knew, and the last thing I wanted to do was put Skye, her boutique, or myself in danger. I mean, he just wanted answers, right? I was sure at this point we could have a civilized conversation. We had been talking business for a few weeks now, trying to build some type of comradery. Surely, we could talk about our dead loved ones. I had the perfect setup in mind, and I knew Vice's dumb ass would fall for it.

Finally, after tossing it around in my head for days, I went ahead and gave Goon a call. I mean, fuck it. All I could do was try to give this man a reason to get some sleep at night. The phone rang a few times before he answered, and I was nervous I would lose the nerve to say something to him.

"Talk to me," he answered, sounding like he was outside. I could hear cars and other sounds in the background.

"Hey, Charles . . . I mean, Goon. I know you told me to call you that before," I laughed, correcting myself before he had the chance. He laughed a little as well, putting me in a better place.

"Hey, Selah. What can I do for you?"

"Do you have time for a quick conversation?"

"I do actually. Let me get these groceries in the car. Just hold on one second."

I listened as he rustled the bags around, getting everything inside. I only heard one door open and close, so I assumed he was by himself. Once he got settled, he came back to the call.

"Okay, sorry about that. What's going on?"

"I think I may have some information for you regarding Chase and those calls you've been getting," I responded while I still had the nerve. I wasn't sure how I was going to spin this shit, but I was pretty good at making shit up along the way.

"Say word?"

"Word," I responded.

"Well, shit, drop some knowledge on me."

"Okay, so here's what I know. . . ."

I fed him this story that the calls he was receiving were coming from the ex-friend of Chase's girlfriend, who was my sister. Shit, it wasn't a complete lie. I came to find out I was the side chick, much to my dismay. I told him that the girl's name was Teresa. There are a billion bitches in the hood with that name. They'd be trying to find a needle in a haystack trying to match that name to a face. I wasn't sure how she got Chase's phone, but she had been trying to extort me for money as well since Chase's death. I finally got to place a face with the voice, and she was some random girl I knew from around the way.

"A real hood booga-ass bitch," I said, throwing some stank on her name.

"Wow, do you have a pic? She's had a price on her head for months. I can send the goons over there tonight," he said, surprisingly calmer than I thought he would be.

"No need for that. I'm already on it. Give me some time. I already have something in the works. I'll text you once the deed is done. I'll handle it. Trust me on this."

"Ma, tell me you not out here bustin' guns. Y'all don't even seem like the type," he tossed out, clearly underestimating us. They always did until the bullet was inches from their skull.

"I'm not saying all that. Just let me handle it. If by chance I can't, I'll give you what you need to put the word out."

"Okay. I'll let you do what you do. Get at me."

"Will do."

After I hung up with him, I went down to the boutique to have a word with Renee. When I got there the store was poppin', and the fashionistas were handling their business. I stopped at the door and just smiled as I watched them work their magic. Skye should be proud of what she built, and I couldn't wait for her to get back so that she could submerge herself in it.

"Hey, Renee, when you get a minute meet me in the back." She nodded her head to acknowledge me as she finished up with her client. It was now time to see if she would hold up her end of the bargain.

Shortly after, she was in the office, looking like she was nervous. She sat quietly while I finished up a call with my Realtor. I was so ready to get this shit with Vice done and over with that I could hardly concentrate on the conversation.

"Thanks, Renee, sorry for the holdup. I see it's rocking out there today."

"Yes, indeed! I spoke with Skye earlier on FaceTime. That little boy is so handsome," she gushed as she made herself comfortable. Renee was okay with me. She hadn't proved to be shady just yet, but we'd see eventually. Folks always showed their true colors.

"Truth. So you remember what we discussed?" I asked, making sure to maintain eye contact to see if she got shifty.

"I do."

"It's time to put it in motion."

"I'm already on it. I'm supposed to be meeting up with her tonight. I got you."

"Perfect. Let the games begin."

Chapter 28

Vice

Move in Silence

Hey, girl. Can I meet up with you later today? I left my keys at your house, and the store key is on there. The pink one. I'm off today, but I'll need them for tomorrow.

I read the text, and the smile that spread across my face was bigger than the Grinch right after he stole Christmas from Whoville. No way was my luck this damn good. Did the keys literally just fall into my damn lap? I got up to go look, and sure enough her keys were sticking out from the side cushion on the couch. They must have fallen out when we were drinking and smoking last night.

Oh, shit, how did you get in your house? I texted back as I began to get dressed. I had to hurry up and make a copy of the key before she came and picked them up.

I had a spare key in my glove compartment. I didn't feel like driving all the way back to your house. I was already buzz driving, and the cops were out heavy last night.

Her drunk ass told me everything I needed to know to get into the damn store. I had been juicing her for information for weeks. The Fashion District didn't open to the public until 10:00 a.m. However, the shop owners could use their key to get into the mall before hours to get their store ready for the day. Security did rounds every hour starting an hour before the mall opened. That meant that as long as I got there before 9:00 a.m., no one would see me. I planned to get there no later than 7:00 a.m. That way it would be still kind of dark out, and no one would really see me. This was perfect! She told me they had been keeping the money in the safe in Skye's office, only making the drop once a week because they really didn't have time.

"On any given day, there's about fifteen thousand dollars in cash on the premises. Twin comes to make the drops for the store," she offered, talking about Selah.

"Yeah? When is the next drop?"

"Friday morning," she slurred as she tipped the cup to her lips again. This shit was too damn easy. Now when you got millions, $15,000 ain't a whole lot, but that wasn't the point. I was about to clean that entire back out and dip on they asses. At the end of it all, friendship isn't always what it's cracked up to be. I promise this is the entire truth. The same ones who ride with you will ride right by you when they got all they need from you. I didn't think it would take me until adulthood to figure that shit out, but better late than never. For me, it wasn't about the money. It was the principle and a lesson that needed to be taught. Don't bite the hand that helps you hide bodies. I wasn't concerned getting caught or losing their friendship because I knew they would never find me, and whatever we had left had fizzled out a long time ago. I finally got a little apartment in the country and was planning to move this coming weekend anyway. They'd never be able to find me.

Okay, just let me know when you're on your way. I'm on my way to the market. I'll let you know once I'm back, I texted back as I hopped into my car.

I jetted across the city to Parkside to get a copy of the key made at Lowe's. I got a copy of all the damn keys because I didn't know what all opened up what at the store. I noticed three of the keys had these rubber rings around them. I guessed that was how she identified store keys from house keys. By the time she came to get the keys, I had already made my copies and was plotting my arrival.

We chopped it up a little when she stopped by. I didn't want to seem suspicious. I even invited her in to eat some of the food I had gotten while I was out. I was hoping she would decline, because I didn't want

her to see that I had already started packing. I had to
slide out of the hood undetected. I decided I wouldn't
leave my furniture and hired a moving company to
come get my shit. I could have gotten those fools off
the stoop and paid them, but no one knew where the
bat cave was but Batman. You dig?

We talked a little more, and then she was on her
way, stating that she wanted to rest up before she had
to go back in the next day. Once those doors opened,
it was nonstop for them until closing, so a good
night's rest was recommended. I closed my door and
went back to packing. I was contemplating taking
someone with me, but who? I couldn't carry all that
shit out by myself. Honestly, did I really need the
clothes? In her drunken stupor, Renee gave me
the damn code to the safe, so this shit was going to be
easy as fuck. As the day went on, I thought about it,
and just cleaning the safe out would be enough. She
would need the merchandise to bounce back from the
hit she was about to take.

I couldn't even sleep on Thursday night. I was so
fucking nervous. This shit was just too damn easy,
and I couldn't help but wonder why. I mean, Renee
could never hold shit, so I wasn't surprised that
she was dropping tea about the business like she
was. Every time she gave me information, I gave her
money. She'd already gotten about $50,000 from me
so far. She couldn't help me rob the store because
she worked there, so that would just be odd. When I

gave her the first bit of money, she questioned what it was for.

"I know you saw what's in that safe," I responded, giving her a knowing look. She returned the same look letting me know she had. "It looks like a lot, but it's really just a bunch of small bills. My only request is that it stays between me and you. I don't need the hood on my top, dig me?" I said to her as I slid the envelope across the table.

"What safe?" she responded as she pocketed the money.

"Exactly."

I was dressed in all black with huge sunglasses on. I grabbed a cheap wig from the hair store, and I just hoped I did a good job covering my identity. There was definitely surveillance in the Fashion District. They were not about to just pick me out in a lineup. They'd have to search for this new bitch I would transform into.

Just as I'd planned, I was down at the District at seven on the dot. I didn't have any issues getting into the entrance from the train, and I made sure to lock the door so that no one would follow me in. When I got to the store, I was able to unlock the gate and successfully punch in the code that Renee gave me to silence the alarm. I pulled the gate back down but didn't lock it so that I could get out easily. I was hoping the door that I saw in the back led to the out-side, but when I walked around the building, I didn't see any door that said 1212A. I saw other numbers, but none that matched, and I was too scared to try the doors to see where they led.

As I made my way to the back of the store, I grabbed a duffle bag off of the display to put the money in. I wasn't sure how much money was back there, but I knew if I could help it, I wouldn't leave a dime of it in there. I felt like I was really getting away with some shit. When I got to the back it took me a second, but I finally found the light switch. When I flipped it on, I saw that everything was covered in plastic. That shit was weird, but whatever. I was just there to get the money.

I made my way back to the safe that was in the back of the office just like Renee said it would be. My fingers started trembling as I punched the code in. I couldn't believe this shit was actually happening. A soft beep and a green light indicated that I had gotten in. Standing back up, I took a deep breath and opened the safe. To my surprise, this bitch was empty. Not a damn dime was in this motherfucker. Oh, the heat that rose through my body couldn't be explained. Renee was going to get her ass beat for this one. When I turned around, I almost shit on myself. There at the door stood Selah, Skye, and Renee. This bitch set me up.

"You know Vice," Skye began as she walked toward me.

I immediately got into a stance to fight. These bitches would have to drag me out of here if they thought they were just going to jump me.

"I wanted to believe you were better than this. We loved you."

"Since when? I was always second best to you bitches." I was about to make a run for it. They would have to catch me first.

Just as she got to her desk, I took off toward her like a running back trying to knock the wind out of her. I didn't make it far. Just as my body collided with hers, I saw the spark from the silencer. Then everything went pitch black. I watched as my body crumpled and hit the floor, landing haphazardly. I looked around the room and saw Renee's arm go down, and she pointed the gun to the floor. As my soul began to ascend, I watched the ladies fold me in half and wrap the shit out of me with plastic and duct tape. I guess the body is more bendable when you're unconscious. I didn't know death would be like this. I didn't even know I would still be having these feelings, but I was ready to meet my fate. I'd catch those bitches the minute they landed in hell with me.

Chapter 29

Selah

Welcome to Motherhood

"Dig just a little deeper. I gotta be sure this bitch doesn't pop back up on us. We don't need a repeat of what happened before," Selah said as we dug a grave for Vice. I wasn't upset about digging this grave at all. I couldn't even believe it even came to this, but it just went to show that friendship ain't always what you think it should be.

We went there to kill her. This was the first time ever where our true intent was to take somebody out. Kevin, Chase, Sajdah—they were all accidents. This one was intentional. The night before the store was closed, Selah and Renee made sure to cover the entire office in thick plastic, and all of the clothing and baby stuff were moved to the little storage room where the shoes were kept. We came there to kill her.

That was the only way she would be leaving there. My son was with his aunt for the night while Selah and I put things in motion.

Selah moved quicker than I thought she would. When I spoke with Goon again about the store, he mentioned that Selah had contacted him about a possible lead on who killed Chase. I assured him that if she said she had it handled, her word was bond. We talked figures and first-month sales, and surprisingly he was ready to fly back out so that we could incorporate his brand with mine. It made me sad that we were kind of deceiving him with not telling the entire truth about who we were, but for his sake it was better that way. He didn't need to compromise his career for Vice's dumb ass.

I had been feeling uncomfortable and getting nervous about the baby. It was like he was in there practicing karate moves. When I went to my last appointment, he was practically at the damn opening. My doctor didn't think I would last the entire forty weeks, and I was okay with it. I had decided to stay home on this particular day. I just couldn't bring myself to get out of the bed and travel. My stomach felt so heavy, and I was scared. The amount of pressure I was feeling in my vagina had me on edge. Luckily, Selah came to stay over the night before. She refused to leave me by myself for too long. I hated it, but I was glad she was there at the same time.

"Girl, I'm not leaving you in here by yourself and this damn baby show up. Chill. I can get back home whenever," she said as she made herself comfortable on the other side of the bed. I had a guest room, mind you, but she insisted on sleeping in the same bed as me. I gave that argument up a long time ago. When I got up to go to the restroom, the pressure seemed to increase. I emptied my bladder, but water kept pouring out.

"Selah! Selah!" I yelled from down the hall. I could hear her jumping out of bed and racing toward me. "I think my water broke!" I immediately started crying. I did not want to have my baby on the toilet. Thank God she insisted on staying. I would have been in a total panic if I were here by myself.

"Okay, we got this. Is it still a lot or did it slow down?" she asked as she turned the sink on and grabbed a rag from the basket. I knew this bitch didn't think she was about to wash me up.

"I don't know," I said, my nerves taking over.

"Did the plug come out?"

"Plug? What the fuck are you talking about?"

"Your mucus plug. It usually releases once the water breaks, I think."

"Bitch, I don't know!" I began to cry hysterically, but she didn't seem fazed at all. You'd have thought she'd done this a time or three.

"Okay, stand up slowly. You are going to get washed and put on a pad. I'll put some towels in the seat of the car. We are going to get you to the hospital. Did you pack a baby bag?"

"Yes, it's in the closet downstairs."

"Okay, cool. I'll get everything ready. You get cleaned up. I see your mucus plug in the toilet. A baby is on the way, bitch!"

I did as I was instructed, making sure to keep time of the contractions that I was starting to experience. I was so not ready for this. Everything seemed to move in a blur as she came to help me get dressed and ushered me out of the house into her car. Thank God for leather seats. She joked on the way to the hospital that I owed her a car detail after this. This felt like the longest ride of my life, and I just squeezed my legs closed so that the baby wouldn't come out in the car. Yeah, I was being dramatic because I didn't know what the hell was happening. I just knew I was about to meet my child soon, and that shit scared me more than anything else.

When we got inside, I was whisked away to labor and delivery, where my doctor met me. They hooked me up to monitors to make sure the baby and I were okay, and now we played the waiting game. I'd never had so many people poking and prodding in my coochie in my life! Every damn body just kept looking and poking around. After a while you just give up all modesty. I texted Rynisha, my baby father's sister, to let her know I was in labor at the hospital, and she was hype as shit and on her way.

We had grown a little bond over the last few months. Even her mom stopped with the threats, even though she still gave me the side-eye when I saw her. I thought I was just going to go in and push this baby out, but this little bugger was stubborn and kept me in labor for twenty-three whole hours! That is a horrible feeling, just in case you were wondering. It wasn't until the wee hours of the morning that I started to get some action. I finally was able to fall asleep, but all of a sudden I got this overwhelming feeling to poop. Like, what the hell was this?

"Selah, can you grab the nurse?" I called out to her sleeping form in the reclining chair across from me. Rynisha was in the other chair near the door.

"What's wrong? Is the baby coming?" she asked, jumping up and coming to my side. Rynisha did the same.

"I don't think so. I just feel like I need to take a shit."

"Bitch, don't push! The baby is coming!" Rynisha ran out to the hall to grab the nurse from the station. When she came in with my midwife, they checked, and sure enough I was dilated ten centimeters, and my baby was in position in the birthing canal, about to make an appearance. I honestly didn't feel any pain, just a bunch of pressure. That epidural was definitely doing what it was supposed to do. Selah held one leg, and Rynisha held the other as I prayed and breathed through the push. The fourth push was the charm, and shortly after, I heard my baby cry.

The tears, I couldn't stop them. This moment right here was as perfect as I could expect, and I was so grateful I didn't have to do this by myself.

"It's a boy," the midwife announced as the nurse cleaned my baby up while we pushed again to get the afterbirth out. Rynisha asked her to save it so that she could dehydrate it and make pills for me to take.

"Sis, I'm not taking no afterbirth pills," I said, frowning my face up.

"Of course you are. It has some great nutrients for you and the baby. Trust me on this. I've done this four times."

The nurse came over and placed my baby in my arms, and he immediately latched on to my breast. I was in awe of his little body. I pulled the blanket back to examine his body. I had to make sure he had all ten fingers and toes. Gosh, he looked just like his dad! I was so sad he wasn't here for this, but it was okay. I was going to make sure his son knew how amazing he was.

We spent the weekend in the hospital, he was circumcised, and they kicked us out by noon on Monday. I was a mom with a real baby. I still couldn't believe it. The first week home was wild. I wanted to go to the store and work, but I just pushed a baby out of my ass a few days ago, so I went ahead and sat my ass down. Dave's mom came over, and I was a little afraid that she would keep her word and beat my ass now that the baby was out. We were a little village in there: me, Selah, Rynisha, and her mom making sure the baby and I were good. The baby's room was set up and ready to go when I got home. Selah must have done that when she left the hospital to go home and freshen up. When she came back, Rynisha left and did the same thing. I was so grateful for everything these ladies were doing for us, and for the first time, I felt like I really had a family.

Renee was great at keeping me posted on what was going on at the store. Business was still booming, and everyone was still getting along. We did a few FaceTimes so the staff could see the baby, and before I knew it, my little man was 3 weeks old. I only planned to stay out for six weeks, but if Renee kept moving how she was moving, I thought I may take a little more time off. I was not putting my baby in daycare, so Selah set up a little nursery area in the office for me so that when I got back I had somewhere to put him. I really could do what I did from home, but she knew how I was. I needed to be out and about.

"So it's time to get that bitch," Selah said to me over breakfast at my house one morning. She got in the kitchen and whipped us up a meal that would make her mother proud: peach cobbler pancakes, beef sausage, and the fluffiest cheese eggs I'd ever had. That orange juice hit the spot, too. While my

baby got milk wasted, I chatted with my friend, my sister, about what we had to do. Rynisha and her mom finally went home and promised to check in on me periodically.

"Yeah?"

"Yeah. I low-key got Renee on board to help with the setup. Vice wants us dead. Shit fell flat with what she was trying to do with Goon, so now she's gunning for us. Renee told me she's planning to hit the boutique this week. She's so slow she doesn't even realize she's walking right into her death."

"You're going to kill her?" I asked, still not believing that we were even at this state with our friend. We came from grade school together. It wasn't supposed to end like this.

"She's going to die. Don't worry about the how. Just see if Rynisha wouldn't mind babysitting on Thursday. I know you don't want to be away from your son, but we need to handle this quickly."

Friday got here before we knew it. Selah spoke to my favorite security guard friend to help us out. All she needed him to do was make sure the cameras near the store and the loading dock stopped working from 5:00 to 8:00 a.m. They didn't start rounds until 9:00. We didn't want any footage of either of us coming or going. Renee had already set the trap. We just had to wait for Vice to show up.

She showed up right on time. We were hiding in the bathroom with the door cracked and the lights out so that she couldn't see us when she came in. Now this is where greed makes you blind. She had been in the back of the store before. She didn't think it was odd that all of a sudden everything was covered in plastic? Or maybe she just didn't care. Her eyes were on the safe. She had to have felt dumb as shit when she opened it and saw it empty. Selah made the drop the day before to be on the safe side. We were not about to take any Ls this season.

Real shit, I wanted to know, why? I wanted answers, damn it! Why would she turn on us like this? My emotions took over, and I approached her. This ho ran at me like a fucking wild buffalo, and before I could react, I saw the spark . . . and then her body drop. I looked down, and it was a square shot to the forehead. She was gone.

I didn't even freeze. I immediately jumped into action as we folded her body in half at the waist and wrapped her tightly in the plastic. Then we taped it and stuffed her into an oversized duffle bag. I didn't know where Selah got that shit from, but I didn't ask any questions. We used the dolly to roll her out to the loading dock area and stuck her body in the trunk of the rental. Selah drove the car down to the bottom and parked it near our makeshift graveyard. We would put her in the earth once the sun went down.

We went back into the store and made sure everything was back the way it was supposed to be, locking the gates back up like we were never even *there. All of this happened in a twenty-minute time span, down to the minute just like we planned. As promised, I gave Renee the contents of the safe that were promised to her. I still had a spare key to her apartment from back when we were cool. Luckily, she didn't change the locks. We gloved up before going inside just to be on the safe side. We didn't think anyone would look for her, but you never know these days. When we got inside it looked like she was packing to move, but the safe was cracked open a little. Renee offered me half the money, and we agreed to split it down the middle and never speak of it again. She also helped herself to a few of the designer purses that Vice had accumulated, and left the rest.*

"See you at ten?" she asked as she got in her car to head home.

"I'll be in around noon. I need a nap after this."

"Agreed."

When I got back to the store, it was like nothing ever happened. My fashionistas were busy restocking the racks, and Renee was going over the books from the day before. I ran into my security guard friend and gave him half of what I got out of Vice's safe. He assured me that he was the last one on duty for the night and made sure the entire camera room was unplugged before he left. Honestly, if anyone wanted to break into the mall last night, that would have been the perfect opportunity. Not a damn thing was caught on film. His supervisor called and aired his ass out when they came in the morning and saw everything unplugged. I wasn't sure what excuse he gave them, but I told him if they got too funky, I would gladly hire him to secure my store.

I could tell when I saw him later in the day that he didn't give a fuck what those people had to say. The contents of that envelope were heavy, definitely more than he would make in this year. When I got back home, I took the opportunity to get a good nap in since my son was with his aunt.

Later that night, after we put Vice in the ground and got rid of the evidence, I vowed that I was done with all of this type of shit. Selah made the same promise. Now was the time to step into our purpose and build generational wealth like the queens we were.

Chapter 30

Goon

Tying Up Loose Ends

It's done. Now we can move on with business.

I got the text around 2:00 a.m. from Skye telling me that they had handled the situation. I never really got full closure on this entire Chase murder, but I felt a little better that someone paid for what they had done to my brother. At this point I was ready to just get back to living. I felt like I'd been sitting stagnant for way too long.

Placing the phone back down, I reached over and pulled my wife closer to me as gently as I could. When I got back from Philly, I spoke to her about making it official. It was time to stop playing games and make her an honest woman.

"I understand if you want to go all out for a wedding. Or we can just go right down to the justice of the peace and make it happen. I love you. I want this to be a forever thing."

She sat down and held her growing belly, and I promised I was prepared to go to the ends of the earth for her. I would do whatever she needed me to do. I just wanted her happy. After contemplating for a few minutes, she looked up at me with tears in her eyes.

"You know what? Let's do it. I'm just asking that you fly out your grandmother and my mom and sister so that we can have their blessing."

I got on the phone immediately to give my grandma the news as I heard her speaking with her family. Marriage wasn't about the wedding. It was about the love between two people. In Miami, it wasn't a drawn-out process to get the marriage certificate. We went down to the courts and filed for the paperwork, and they gave us sixty days to make it official. I called my grandmother and told her to bring Mrs. Garret, who was my grandma's best friend and just happened to be an officiant. I called my travel agent, and within thirty days we were married on the beach in Nassau, Bahamas, in front of the people who loved us the most. It felt amazing to be in love, and for once in my life everything felt complete. As I watched her belly grow over the next few months, I knew there was nothing I wouldn't do to protect her. She was my rock. She'd been here since the beginning.

I even managed to get business going with Selah and Skye on two separate business ventures. Selah had this amazing idea called All the Rage. It was a themed rage room where people could come throw axes, smash TVs, and chill, eat, and drink in one setting. Her Philly location was doing well, and I was helping her set up her Miami location.

Skye assisted me in opening After Dark: a men's clothing brand that was the perfect complement to her women's line. The store layout was similar, and it offered nice, high-end pieces for the corporate man who knew how to turn up.

When my baby made her appearance, I vowed to be the best father I knew how to be, and I thanked God for another chance at love, life, and happiness. Life was good, and I couldn't ask for anything more.

Chapter 31

Selah

The Bitch Is Dead

To say peace of mind was priceless is an understatement. It'd been eons since I could live and not look over my shoulder. I finally closed on my house, and I had Nafisa find me a warehouse that I could turn into my rage room, and business was going well. I had peace. Finally.

I also had love, however short-lived that would be. I never thought I would find it again, and at one point I thought my prayers were going unanswered. So I met this guy, and at first it wasn't anything. I met him on a trip to Lowe's when I was looking at appliances for my new house. He owned a landscaping business and offered me a card in case I needed any work done. I looked him up, and he indeed had a legit business with a good following. I hired him for some services, and we got to talking. You know how it goes.

Things were going well until one day I got a call from a female who told me that he belonged to her. *Here we go with this shit again. I don't know why men find it so hard to be faithful.* I mean, I'd like to think I was pretty dope. I didn't know what the problem was with these guys. I asked him, he lied, I poisoned him. The end. I said I wouldn't shoot anyone else. There's a million ways to kill a motherfucker that doesn't involve gunfire.

Long story short, he was in the basement and I was waiting for the cement to dry. I was not playing with these dudes no damn more. I spoke to my therapist about our breakup, and I was just dealing with it one day at a time. There was someone out there for me. I believed it.

"We are made to be in pairs, Selah," my therapist told me as we closed our last session. "God has someone He prepared just for you. He will send him once you are ready to receive him, and not a minute sooner. Just be patient and keep working on yourself. You got this."

As I finished the rest of my wine, I made sure the house was locked up, making a mental note to call and have my number changed in the morning. Sis kept calling, and unless she wanted to join his ass in the other wall in the basement, she'd go ahead about her business. When I got upstairs and turned on the television, his face popped up on the news. His family had been looking for him for a few weeks now, and they were begging anyone to call or give tips if they had seen him.

"Good luck with that," I said to the television as I made myself comfortable in bed. I said Vice was the last one, but sometimes you have to do what you have to do. I picked up this book I had been reading, and it made me think. Was I a serial killer low-key? After careful thought, I decided I wasn't and went ahead and turned the lights out. Now was not the time to dwell in negativity. The New Year was approaching, and I was ready to walk into my purpose.

Whatever that was.

The End

For real this time . . . I think.